COGNITIVE
BREACH

A GENESIS PROJECT NOVELLA

MARK P.J. NADON

Thrillers by Mark P.J. Nadon

<u>**Military Thrillers:**</u>

The Genesis Project

The Genesis Project (Book 1) – June 2024

Monsoon Rendezvous Novella (Book 1.5) – January 2025

Cognitive Breach Novella (Book 1.75) – February 2025

Short Stories

Operation Sanitation – August 2024

Operation Tangle – September 2024

<u>Post Apocalyptic Thrillers:</u>

Armageddon's Descendants Trilogy

The Collective (Book 1) – March 2025

The Chosen (Book 2) – Forthcoming Summer 2025

The Reckoning (Book 3) – Forthcoming Winter 2026

Cognitive Breach (A Genesis Project Novella)

Visit the author's website at www.markpjnadon.ca

Cover designed by MiBlart

First Published: February 2024

ISBN (Electronic Book): 978-1-7383077-8-4
ISBN (Paperback): 978-1-7383077-9-1

For my son Matthew—may you always
have the courage to bring light to dark places.

Chapter 1
Sunday

Captain David Guarnere ran his fingers along the top of his silk dress shirt, feeling the silver locket strung around his neck. He knew the tiny words etched on it by touch: *Keep dancing*. Even when the music stops. It was his sister's favorite saying. But she'd stopped dancing.

Brigadier General Korhonen stood looming over David from the head of a large oak table ten yards away, a white screen behind him taller than he was. He probably had no idea how to use it. The mission briefing was coming together too rapidly for a PowerPoint, anyway. Since it was Sunday and everyone at the table had been called in for an emergency briefing, all the techs were at home. The last time his superiors had put something together this quick, people had died, and they'd covered up the conspiracy. Blake had done all the killing then, taking out the Genesis Project trash. Those who talked about it in secret nicknamed it Operation Mindwarp. There was nearly no paper trail outside of whatever was locked away in the archive.

Blake, aka Master Chief Powell, sat beside him with General Bradford and Major Lokey seated on the opposite side. David was the only person in the room that hadn't seen active combat, though he'd seen plenty of dead bodies in nightmares just as real in the Genesis.

There was something about knowing in the back of his mind it wasn't happening to him that kept him sane. He gave a quick once-over to Blake dressed in combats and swiping the screen on his phone. David wondered how he could sit there looking disinterested after everything he'd been through. Blake was built different. Special ops guys always were.

"I'm giving Captain Guarnere the lead on this mission," General Korhonen said, his thin eyebrows popping up and down like they were throwing punches at anyone who dared question him. As if his physiology overheard, David felt sweat drip from his armpits down his side. It would add nicely to the mixed smells of cologne, BO, and fat-cat cancer sticks in the room.

"Sir, I'm—"

General Korhonen's eyebrows locked in a low position. "Happy to do your job, as ordered?"

David risked a glance around the room. He wasn't imagining it. All their eyes were on him. Blake might have been holding back a smirk. *Bastard knows I shouldn't be taking the lead on special projects.*

"Master Chief, you'll be his second in command." General Korhonen picked up a folder from the table and slammed it back down. "This is a major opportunity for Genesis to prove itself as more than a tool to resolve post-traumatic stress. Nobody has more experience in dream analysis and research than David. And given the case, none of our other operators are...so civilian. I expect you'll be seen as less of a threat."

Nobody in the room blinked. David's mouth hung open, his mind searching for a reason to prove he shouldn't be in command. He'd never been a leader, and he was completely fine with that. The medals and heroics were for guys like Blake. If they wanted him to wear combats, they should have told him to. They weren't nearly as comfortable as Hugo Boss.

"Sir, I understand that—"

General Korhonen went on like David hadn't spoken. "There are more initials attached to this investigation than there are states. FBI, DHS, ATF, NSA are just a few. And none of them got shit in two days of questioning her." He flipped open the folder and tossed a thin stack of paper at everyone at the table. Every stack had the same face on the front: a Caucasian woman with light brown hair and warm blue eyes. Printed at the bottom of the photo was the name Doctor Lena Kurov.

David almost laughed at the contrast between all the US agencies involved and this cute young woman who looked as dangerous as a puppy.

"Not a single military acronym in your examples, sir," Blake said, drumming the table with his fingers to the beat of a song only he knew—maybe "Fortunate Son." He'd picked up the habit in the last few months. His therapist, Doctor Kendra, had suggested it as a solution to blurting out what he actually thought. Every time he played his fingers, David could only imagine what was going through his mind.

Major Lokey glared at Blake like he wanted to pounce on his hand.

"It's not a military operation. I pulled a few strings with a couple of friends just to be considered for this, with all the agencies fighting for lead in the case." General Korhonen cleared his throat and took a sip of water from the glass on the table. "A spy inside the DHS got wind of a planned terrorist operation to bomb an unknown location. When DHS searched the property, they found all the makings of a bomb, but no bomb."

"And a woman," Blake said.

"Yes, and Doctor Kurov sleeping in a bed in an upstairs bedroom. She's not cooperating, despite some *unethical* interrogations." General Korhonen spoke like the Genesis hadn't just finished one of the largest immoral coverups in military history.

David did a double-take of Doctor Kurov's photo. She didn't look like a woman that planted bombs, or withstood interrogation. Maybe they'd failed to get information out of her because she didn't have information to give. "So, we're going into her dreams to see if we can find the target, the bomb, the terrorists, or all three."

"That's correct." General Korhonen said. "If we can use Genesis for interrogation without wasting time or causing her unnecessary harm and trauma, we'll have more budgeting dollars than any other acronym in the forces. Make no mistake, I want all three."

Time, ethics, and money. Especially money. David missed Colonel Marks just a little. The Genesis project leadership, primarily DARPA—Defense Advanced Research Projects Agency, responsible for the advancement of technology within the military—had removed Colonel Marks from command after a fiasco involving dream manipulation. Colonel Marks caused the death of an untold number of people, some by Blake's hand, after the Colonel convinced Blake a terrorist had killed his daughter. But at least Colonel Marks was motivated to help soldiers. After his son was murdered by one of his own men suffering from PTSD, the Colonel made ending PTSD his life's work. Unfortunately, some of his decisions had come at a tremendous cost. General Korhonen was all about budget and crossing all the necessary *t*'s to maximize funding, as if that money was being transferred to his personal bank account.

Blake continued to tap a tune on the table as he scanned the papers, flipping faster than he could possibly read.

"Familiarize yourself with the details." General Korhonen scanned the documents like he, too, was seeing them for the first time. David realized the general meant now and started browsing.

They had little to go on. The files mostly contained large pictures of electrical parts David assumed had something to do with creating a bomb. The profile on Doctor Kurov read like a resume of her accomplishments in AI research. Her doctorate was in computational neuroscience, but David skimmed past the university names, more interested in her publications on autonomous systems. A few documents in the package included articles she'd written: "The Potential of Autonomous Systems," "The Role of AI in Modern Warfare," "The Future of AI Research." David didn't have time to read the details of the articles, but the opening statements read like someone supporting the military, not preparing acts of terrorism. *What had flipped her switch?* Assuming they weren't wrong about her and she wasn't just in the wrong place at the wrong time.

David skimmed through Doctor Kurov's academic background again. And again, all he found was pure research in computational neuroscience and AI systems—complex work that seemed far removed from building bombs in an apartment. None of her published papers hinted at extremist leanings or anti-government views.

"Her background doesn't fit the profile," David said.

Blake glanced up from his phone. "Smart people snap too."

"Maybe. But something's missing here."

"She's brilliant, stubborn, and very capable of following through." General Korhonen said.

"Sounds like my ex-wife." General Bradford chuckled. "Doesn't look much like her, though. Too bad. Might have kept her around longer."

David had never heard a ranking officer speak so frankly, like he was one of the guys at the Saloon. The thought of the rundown bar made David crave a beer. Maybe two or three. He'd planned his day so perfectly, spending all of it with Helen and the boys, but now he had the impression his plans were on hold—indefinitely.

"Any timeframe on when we expect the bomb to go off?"

General Korhonen took a deep breath. "We have nothing. Could be in an hour. Hopefully we have more time than that. The FBI said with the trash they found, the time they'd spent building the bomb, and the bomb now likely in transport, it's not looking good. Any timeframe is a guess, but they suspect it's going off in the next few days."

"FBI? I thought the DHS did the investigating," Blake said, shaking his head and dropping the file hard on the table as if he'd read it thoroughly, though he'd only given it a cursory glance. "Too many moving parts."

Major Lokey grumbled. "Focus on your job as *number two*, Master Chief. Don't worry about civilian agencies." Major Lokey spoke like he was talking to a toddler having suddenly seen a train set while playing with trucks.

Blake's face turned red, and David put his arm out as if to hold Blake down in his chair and gave a quick shake of his head. *Now's not the time.* Those two had hated each other ever since Major Lokey fought for Colonel Marks to stay with the project.

"What do we know about the spy that fed us this information?" David said, hurrying to change the subject and shift Blake's focus to anywhere but Major Lokey.

"Nothing yet. The boots on the ground at DHS don't want us involved, so they're dragging their feet. Even with the National Security Advisor's orders, the usual interagency cooperation has gone dark on this one. They're holding out. You can always make a few calls, but don't count on it." General Korhonen checked his watch. David imagined he had other places to be. Time was money for him.

"So we have no idea what this is about, who is involved, or the target or timeframe. Essentially, the only thing we have is Doctor Kurov." David didn't bother to hide the disbelief in his tone. Not only did he not want to lead this mission, but there was almost no mission to lead. Going into her dreams with no focus was like throwing darts in the dark with no idea where the dart board might be located, or if there even was one. This was Blake's type of mission. David opened his mouth to repeat his objection that he be primary, then closed it. An officer as high ranked as those in the room would stubbornly uphold their decision for the sake of not appearing wrong, even if that decision wasn't best for the mission.

David followed up with a few more questions about the case and didn't get any helpful responses. Mission pretty much impossible was being placed on him, and many people's lives were in the balance. When the officers left the room, Blake smiled and smacked David on the back of the shoulder.

"Well hoorah, Davy. How do you want to tackle this? I was thinking tha—"

"I need to take some time to read through the documents. We aren't rushing into this half-cocked." David paused for a breath as he saw Blake's smile fade. David wasn't ready for the hammer, and all Blake saw were nails. Still, he had to give him something to do, and since he was primary, he gave Blake the job he didn't want. "You can get on the phone with whoever in DHS will talk to you. I need to know as much as I can about the intel they received. Glancing at this package, there isn't much to go on. I want to know how the spy found out about the bomb. Who told him? What do they know? There has to be more to go on than this."

Blake nodded. "Copy. What are you going to do?"

"I'm going to talk to Doctor Kurov. I want to know what kind of woman she is. Her picture doesn't jibe with the accusation. Maybe she really doesn't know anything."

"Don't let a beautiful woman waste your time. Her dreams will tell us a lot more than she'll be willing to." Blake took another look at her picture. "Can't imagine what she's been through. She's pretty attractive. Look David, get a feel for her if you want to, but let's get in the Genesis soon and not waste time. You need to get home at some point. Don't need Helen wondering if you're having an affair again." Blake held back a smirk. Helen had nearly lost her mind over a year ago when David took Blake to Tacoma and lied about it to keep it secret. He'd done that for Blake. She'd thought he was covering up an affair. He swore to keep nothing like that from her again, and he hadn't.

"She knows this is an emergency briefing. I'll call her after I see Doctor Kurov. Let's jet."

Chapter 2

David stepped through the metal detector in the second sublevel of the Genesis compound where they detained soldiers charged with criminal activity. Normally, soldiers spent a few weeks having their nightmares catalogued and ranked in order of worst to much worse by the Genesis technology—using a slew of factors like EEG, REM, muscle tension, galvanic skin response, and hormone levels—before an operator entered their nightmares with them and attempted to alter and defuse post-traumatic stress responses. Some officers would even return to duty after receiving treatment.

That was before a corrupt DARPA military leader and the creator of Operation Mindwarp dreamt up their own agendas: an open market selling vengeance-seeking assassins. Soldiers were used for murder by altering their nightmares to include targets they wanted killed. Such technology wasn't supposed to exist, so nobody went to trial after they were busted. David wished he could forget everything he'd seen.

Three doors down, David peered through a slit in the door and saw Doctor Kurov seated on the floor against the far wall with her legs crossed and her eyes closed. Balled fists rested on her lap, the only part of her body that didn't seem relaxed. One small string of fluorescent light covered with a steel cage lit the room, barely bright enough for David to see her face. The bulbs had about as much life left in them as she did if she didn't start talking; someone would beat the truth out of her eventually.

Doctor Kurov's eyes opened and locked on to his, as if she'd sensed him watching her. She looked nothing like her picture. Same facial features, except those eyes…they were icy daggers, cutting through his soul. The light brown hair that had appeared so full of life in her picture was ragged, dark and stringy, like someone had run oil through her hair and hadn't let her wash it out. Despite the low light, he saw a dark bruise beside her eye where she hadn't healed yet. He didn't want to know what the rest of her looked like.

"Going in, sir?" A sergeant stood beside the door, her hands clasped firmly to her sides despite casually distant feet, an odd mix of being at attention and at ease. A pistol rested on the side of her hip. Having a woman watch a woman helped cover any allegations of sexual misconduct, although David knew the term 'thoroughly questioned' in the FBI report carried a wide range of possibilities. Most violated her human rights.

"How's she doing? Just sitting there?"

The sergeant turned toward the door. "Not heard a peep. She's quiet. They're always quiet."

"No screaming to be let out? Asking why she's being held? Demanding a lawyer?"

"Not heard a peep," she droned.

"Thanks." David said half-heartedly. *So, Doctor Kurov is either exhausted from everything she's been through, or she's not innocent and maybe believes the treatment is justified.*

The sergeant unlocked the door and pulled open the latch. Doctor Kurov didn't move as the door swung open, her eyes cutting into David's psyche. How many times in the last minute had she killed him in her imagination? She'd had time for at least one or two. He wondered what method she used. A booby-trapped door? A suicide vest?

"Hello," David carefully approached her, flinching slightly when the door closed with a loud click. Hopefully she hadn't noticed it, though he had a feeling those eyes noticed everything. "I'm David."

He considered the chair a few feet away from her but elected to lower himself on the floor, far enough away to be out of reach, yet not so far that the conversation felt like an interrogation—as if she cared. "How are you doing?"

One of her eyebrows rose and her nose scrunched up. "Wonderful."

"Would you like something to drink? Eat?" He'd planned to go straight into questioning her because he knew she'd be hostile, but his instinct told him in the last second to take a different approach. Probably not one as stupid sounding as that, since he didn't know if he could get her a drink or food—too late.

"A cold beer and chicken salad," she ordered. He deserved the sarcasm, sure, but he also wondered if he could consider it a break in the chink of her armor.

"I'll see what I can do," he said, matching her empty expression. She didn't need to see him as a waste of time. He had to get her to open up. "First, can you tell me what you were doing in that apartment?"

"You don't know? Putting the finishing touches on a bomb."

"Why?"

She finally looked away. David followed her eyes to the floor but found only the cold stone surface. He'd touched on something. The bomb was probably personal, not psychopathic, whether or not she'd built it herself. Because unless Doctor Kurov had already delivered the bomb to the target and was waiting for it to go off, David assumed she wasn't working alone. Someone currently had the bomb and needed to put it into play. Plus, if the bomb was already in place, she would have skipped town or waited near the target location to ensure it went off, not let herself be arrested in the apartment.

Take your time. Don't jump to conclusions.

"To destroy," she said nonchalantly, those icy eyes finding his again. "That's why bombs are built, aren't they?"

"What are you trying to destroy?" David kept his eyes on hers. It gave him a sense of connection, intimacy, that he enjoyed having with people. They opened up to him faster.

"Who are you?"

"David."

"I remember your name. What do you do here?"

He figured to her, a person's identity was wrapped up in their work. *Hers must be. Computational neuroscientist. Math and the brain, right?*

"I study dreams," he said, choosing not to lie to her. He needed her to be honest, and years with his wife had instilled the value of mutual honesty.

Her icy stare thawed slightly, replaced with a more nuanced sarcasm. "You're going to study my dreams? Do I get to lie on a sofa while you dangle a watch from a chain and hypnotize me?"

David gave a small smile, just at the edge of his lip, enough for her to know he'd matched her slight change in emotional state. With a few seconds to consider what he'd tell her, he adjusted his legs to be slightly closer to her. Her blink lasted just long enough for him to know she'd seen the change. "We're using the help of some newly developed technology for a deeper dive into your dreams."

Doctor Kurov pursed her lips. She made a similar leg adjustment, moving slightly further away from him. Not unexpected. He knew it wouldn't be easy to get her to open up.

"Technology for a deep dive?" She tried to hide an intense swallow. Whatever she was up to, she'd been dreaming about it, otherwise she wouldn't be concerned in the slightest. The Genesis would definitely tell him more. "You're going to hurt me?"

There was an innocence in her he suddenly felt connected to—a hairline connection. She was scared. Afraid of more pain. The source of that fear nagged at him; he'd get Blake to ask the FBI what she'd suffered in their custody right after he spoke with DHS. Blake was a hardened personality that other hardasses opened up to. If anyone was going to give information, they'd give it to him, probably to brag. He wondered what she'd been through that was so terrible she thought innocent people deserved to die. Maybe he could reason with her. Everyone had redemptive qualities. They just needed help to pull them out from deep in their soul.

"No, I'm not going to hurt you," he said, his tone firm yet gentle.

"You think you can understand my dreams, Dreamcatcher? Even the most advanced AI can't truly comprehend human consciousness. That's what makes it so dangerous—it acts without understanding."

Dreamcatcher. A Native American concept. Perhaps she saw him as someone filtering out her dreams, catching the bad ones and letting out the good ones. Or maybe she was wordsmithing. David knew how smart she was, so anything she said could have hidden meanings. He catalogued it in his mind, decided he wasn't going to get anything more from her, and stood, taking a few steps backward toward the door.

"We can talk more after you've gotten some rest."

"So you can come for my dreams? Dreamcatcher?"

Exactly. If he could get her thinking about all the things she didn't want him to know, the Genesis would catalogue them that much faster and maybe they could find the bomb in time.

Without another word, he turned, rapped on the door, and left.

Chapter 3

David found Blake on the phone in the operator's office. As he plopped into his chair and leaned back, waiting for Blake's call to end, he ran through his conversation with Doctor Kurov in his mind. It had gone well by his estimation. Tomorrow, he'd be in her dream, and the next time he saw her in confinement, he'd need a cold beer and a chicken salad to win her over to his side. Other agencies probably hadn't played good cop. Not the way he could, by genuinely caring. Although the Genesis would likely play the biggest role in ending this operation, winning her over might help later.

Blake pressed a button on his phone and casually tossed it on his desk. He bent forward and rubbed his eyes. "They wouldn't give me anything. No names, no specifics. Apparently, it could compromise their spy tactics. Figured you'd want me to try a few other agencies, but I got the same stonewalling. All the agencies agree that talking to the military is a potential minefield."

"Minefield?"

"My words. I'm summarizing the last twenty minutes. Any success on your end?" He wheeled over to David. "How's she lookin?"

"Rough. Someone gets full points for treating her like just another criminal."

Blake shook his head, amused. "Not surprised. Learn anything useful?"

"Established the start of a relationship. Might be useful later." David leaned back in his chair, saw Blake's eyebrows raise combined with a sly grin. "Whatever reason she has for being part of this, it's personal. Not just the greater good bullshit. Something happened that devastated her."

Blake reached for his phone, checked it, and threw it back on the table. "Goddamn, Sophia, come on."

"Trouble at home?"

"Fourteen going on thirty. Took a bullet and thinks she's invincible."

David smiled. "She's a good kid. Seemed happy at the party last week."

"Oh yeah?" Blake threw his hands up in the air. "Says the guy who took his wife and kids and left by eight thirty. Sophia got shit-faced, barely able to walk to the bed, and I'm pretty sure made out with that Ethan kid."

"Ethan? The tall kid with cement in his hair?" David laughed. "You'd know if she tried running her hands through that tar. She'd still be stuck to it."

"Clara wants me to talk to her. She tried, and it didn't go so well. Apparently, her little girl acts just like her father." Blake tapped his fingers on the desk, a very different vibe to the tune in the meeting. Maybe heavy metal?

"You don't think Sophia acts like you? Runs headfirst into things without thinking it through? Prefers a sledgehammer to a screwdriver?" David's phone vibrated on the desk. He risked a quick glance between chuckles and saw it was Helen texting him to ask when he'd be home. "Remember the time she tried to fix her lamp light? She thought she stripped the screw, then took a hammer and smashed it open, only to realize she'd tried a hex tip instead of a Phillips? She taped the damn thing back together with duct-tape and used it for another month."

Blake rubbed his beard to hide his smile. "She still uses that light to read books every night. Totally Clara."

"She's home every night, tells you when she gets into trouble, and isn't on any hard drugs or pregnant. A win in my books."

"You and Clara aren't reading the same genre then." Blake said.

They laughed as First Sergeant Martin moseyed into the room and plopped on his chair, dropping hard enough to make David think he'd just taken a round in the chest. "I need a vacation."

"Heard you were working on the Ashford case, spending all your time on the beach," Blake said, tapping his fingers to the tune of "Wipe Out." He'd already found a way to weaponize his therapist's suggestions.

"Son of a bitch," Sergeant Martin leaned forward in his chair, his hands outstretched like Homer Simpson strangling Bart. "That beach incursion you're talking about involved the slaughter of an entire platoon of Navy SEALS."

Blake's smile faded. "Shit, sorry. Didn't realize."

David made an explosion gesture with his hands, then got a whiff of pepper and lavender that must have trailed in after Sergeant Martin and coughed into his hand. Sergeant Martin might think he needed a vacation, but what he definitely needed was a shower to clear out the bath he'd taken in Dior Sauvage.

"Nothing to accomplish tonight. I'll be here first thing in the morning. Have a good night, boys." David tapped Blake's shoulder on his way out of the office. "Not too many at the Saloon old man."

"Hey, congratulations," Sergeant Martin shouted as David stepped through the doorway. "I heard you're number one on an op. If you need a better number two, just let me know."

"Thanks," David said.

A few steps down the hallway, he heard Blake say, "I'm afraid the only number two you'd excel at comes with a roll of toilet paper."

Always the sledgehammer. Never the screwdriver.

***

David sat at the dinner table, using his fork to chase the peas around his plate, more like a game of soccer than a spearing challenge.

"What's on your mind?" Helen worked her fingers through her hair in rapid succession, like it never sat in the right spot.

After a few more flicks of the peas, he placed his fork on the table and found her eyes, the color of autumn leaves touched by sunlight. Forcing a smile wasn't in his relationship playbook, so he tightened his lips—it's how he really felt.

"Work. They made me lead on a project."

Helen smiled. "That's good, isn't it?" She waved a dismissive, playful hand. "Oh, you don't think you want to lead, but you're a good leader. What's the assignment?"

Two years ago, he might have lied to her. But the consequences of keeping things from her only destroyed their relationship, to the point they'd separated for a few months. She'd asked him to leave their family home so she could have some time to think. Those months crawled by, and he realized the job wasn't important enough to him to keep secrets from her. He'd rather lose the job than lose his family. Telling her about the nightmares, the soldiers he worked with, the Genesis Project and what it could really do, and Operation Mindwarp, shook her to her core. Each story he shared left her less surprised but still deeply unsettled. He reminded her that if the events behind the nightmares weren't so traumatic, they wouldn't cause PTSD.

"Need to make sure you keep this one really quiet," he said, glancing around the empty table out of habit. His son Lenny was eating at a friend's house, but he'd be home soon—he preferred being home with his video games than with his friends. That wouldn't last long. Sawyer was likely in his room, although he probably wouldn't be listening even if he were at the table—just like a teenager.

"It's bad," he added.

Helen swallowed so hard the saliva seemed to stall in her throat for a moment before working its way down. "Worse than Mindwarp?"

"Different. The DHS raided a home on a tip from an informant that bombs were being made there. They found components but the bomb had already left. And a woman asleep in bed, who they arrested and didn't treat too well." *Didn't treat too well* was the best truth David could come up with.

Helen rubbed the side of her head, just above her ear. *Stress rising.* "I don't understand. What does the DHS have to do with Genesis? How are you involved?" Her mouth closed as her frown deepened. "They didn't find the bomb? It's out there? It could be anywhere?" Her eyes darted around the room like she might find the bomb sitting in their kitchen.

"The Genesis is logging her dreams. Tomorrow I'm going into them to find out what I can about the bomb. We're hoping there are clues about what they planned to do with it, where it might be, when it might go off...that sort of thing."

Helen groaned. "They finally give you a leadership position on a mission and it's a multi-agency operation with a goddamn bomb? Why you?"

"Why me?" he echoed.

"I didn't mean it like that." She smiled sweetly, hopped off her chair, and gave him a half hug as she dropped into his lap and pressed her lips to his. Her kiss was soft, her lips smooth, more playful than passionate. He wanted more. She pulled away in her evilly tempting way.

"They said it's because of the research I've done on dreams. I figure it has a lot to do with my doctorate in psychology. The others are more—"

"Aggressive?" she answered. "And would have the same tactics as the DHS tough guys, no doubt."

He shrugged. "Not sure it will matter. Her dreams might offer up all the answers I need without trying."

"What's she like? Is she pretty?"

Shots fired. Proceed with caution. Though, he knew better than to hesitate. Worse than saying she was attractive was hesitating to tell the truth. He blurted, "She looked rough. Beat up. At least a day or two of going through FBI or some other agency interrogation tactics. She was probably pretty before they had at her." He knew that was the case from her photo.

Helen raised an eyebrow as if she knew she'd been swindled somehow. He gave her a warm, innocent smile to deflect her growing curiosity and pulled her in for a longer kiss.

"Only eyes for you, sweetheart." And he meant it. She was older than him by age, but only a few light wrinkles gave it away. She'd negotiated favorable terms with time itself. If anything, the light fluff she'd put on since having Lenny six years ago made her look younger.

"I told Lenny we'd go to the mall tomorrow to get him some new shorts and t-shirts. And we have the eclipse on Wednesday. I bribed them both with a visit to Ben & Jerry's. Should we go? What if the bomb is in the mall or at the school?" she asked. How quickly the switch had flipped.

"Not a bad idea to lie low for a few days. Maybe take him to an outlet store with ice cream nearby instead of the mall? The mall's a more likely target than a small clothing store. It wouldn't have enough casualties." They had built the bomb thirty miles away on the outskirts of San Diego. The target could be anywhere. Los Angeles was only 120 miles away. Anaheim was 95 miles. So many cities with large gatherings. *Jesus.*

David closed his eyes and tried to clear his mind. He told himself he'd never take work home and he rarely did. Somehow, he'd always managed to share what he could with Helen about his work, then blocked it out when he hung out with his boys. But this was different. It wasn't one soldier's life on the line. Countless lives could be lost, and the bomb could go off at any time. He could arrive at Genesis tomorrow and be told it already had.

Chapter 4
Monday

The Genesis II lid lay open like a tanning bed, waiting for David to lie down before it dropped on him, pressing the goo into his face and connecting him to Doctor Kurov, who'd be sleeping in another room with a Genesis headset on. Blake hovered over the screen, tapping buttons on the display. David's nerves gave him the energy to keep moving. He hadn't slept at all the night before and had no energy of his own.

"Ready?" he asked Blake as he prepared to drop the gown and lay almost naked on the jelly substance atop the bed. With some of the Genesis upgrades, command felt it was necessary to strip all clothing so the sensors could accurately read vitals. If an operator was in distress, the machine would disconnect automatically. What happened to Blake in Mindwarp wouldn't happen again. At least they let him keep his boxer-briefs on.

"Charlie Mike," Blake said. "I'll have eyes on out here."

The lid dropped over him. Despite the hundreds of times it had pressed against his face and loaded the virtual room, he still cringed, hoping he didn't suffocate.

David snapped his fingers and a light flicked on. It illuminated only the space where he stood. Blackness waited around him, ready to pounce at the opportunity to suck out the light. The menu popped up with two major dream sequences for Doctor Kurov, and three minor. The new AI bot used for dream sorting would have linked the fragments by theme, emotions, and stress impact, offering what it calculated to be the most significant dreams. Minor dreams almost never amounted to anything.

The AI didn't think like a human, though. It was trying to understand a painting by analyzing the chemical composition of the paint—technically accurate but blind to the actual meaning. It would disregard many important nuances, like a keychain around her neck. He felt for his own keychain, knowing it wouldn't be there, but aware of how important it would be in one of his dreams. The AI would prioritize dramatic confrontations and emotional peaks, while overlooking the quiet details that often held real truth. Despite his hesitation, David pressed the first sequence.

***

David stood inside a dilapidated brick building. Bricks were missing from several places in the wall, creating a spyhole to look out of or a peephole to look in from. Doctor Kurov sat on a large rocking chair with two girls in her lap. Her bright eyes held none of the laser-like qualities she'd shown in her cell. One child must have been four years old, clinging to Doctor Kurov's light brown hair like a rope out of a swimming pool. The other girl might have been eight or ten.

Doctor Kurov laughed when the older girl whispered something into her ear. The doctor had a natural beauty about her he bet could be multiplied ten-fold by getting to know her.

Both kids had dark skin—probably not her own, despite their cuddling. She wore tight jeans and a white blouse, very different from the kids who wore mismatched blue, yellow, and red shirts and pants. No shoes. He guessed they were in a foreign country. Maybe she was volunteering, and she'd been there long enough to earn their affection. He'd have Blake look into it later.

He heard a buzzing noise in the distance and assumed they were on a bee farm or a construction site. David expected killer bees to fly out of nooks and crannies, forcing him to exit the dream before being stung to death. That's how nightmares went—never a happy ending. He hated bee stings as much as the next person, and the Genesis didn't pull any punches.

The building shook. David lost his balance. A quick hand on the ground broke his fall. Doctor Kurov pulled the kids in close. Her eyes were wide, scared.

Shouting came from the adjacent room—frantic children and panicked parents. Some parents tried to keep everyone calm, but it wasn't working. They knew something terrible was about to happen. David did too. That's why he was there. He waited for the wind to blow the roof off or a tsunami to flood the room. Even the bees had quieted.

"It's okay. It's going to be okay," Doctor Kurov said, pulling the kids tight to her.

The building shook again. This time, the ceiling collapsed. David leaped out of the way, barely avoiding being crushed. The children sprang from her arms and sprinted for the other room. Doctor Kurov didn't chase them. The other room collapsed.

In a blink, he was outside, the blistering sun instantly making him sweat. Dust clouded his vision, and he coughed violently, nearly vomiting to get the sand out of his throat. "Doctor Kurov?" he shouted instinctively, though he knew she wasn't going to answer. Another fit of coughing. Doctor Kurov had to be nearby; the Genesis never led operators far from the scene, or they'd find themselves in darkness. He waved his hands in the dust, expecting to touch her arm.

As the dust settled, he saw her crawling a few paces away. She spoke too quietly for him to hear. *This is the tragedy that started it all.*

The surrounding buildings were unharmed other than a few gouges to the structure from flying debris. *How did she get out of the room?* Typically, nightmares were linear, reliving specific moments from a soldier's life. This was different because Genesis hadn't had enough time to build the sequence properly. David followed Doctor Kurov as she stumbled toward the rubble. She shouldn't be alive. The explosion had crushed the place they'd stood in moments ago. A child walked past, dazed, calling for her mommy. David's heart broke a little when he imagined Lenny in the girl's place.

Doctor Kurov muttered, limping through the carnage. Dozens of people rushed to help, pulling those still living a safe distance away. Paramedics would arrive soon. They'd get help. Those who could be helped.

He reached Doctor Kurov in a few quick bounds and heard her whispers. "I'm sorry. I'm so sorry." As if she'd levelled the building herself.

"Sorry about what?" he asked, knowing she couldn't hear him and wouldn't respond.

"I'm so sorry."

Did she have something to do with the explosion? No, she wouldn't have held the kids in her arms so lovingly if she'd intended to kill them...would she? Was she suffering from paranoid delusions, thinking they'd be better off dead? She didn't fit the profile. When he'd spoken to her, she'd not claimed to be protecting anyone, or safeguarding people for their own good. There was no record of isolation or erratic behavior in her history, although that didn't mean it wasn't there. No mental health issues, graduating average in her class before excelling in computational research. David hadn't had time to delve deep, but remembered she used computer-based algorithms and data analysis to solve complex problems. It didn't sound like bomb making school. He'd have to read up on it.

The scene went dark.

***

David sat inside the Genesis virtual lobby on a leather armchair. The room was one of his making—neutral ground where he could talk to a client between sessions without exiting Genesis, like the space between thunder and lightning, where time seemed to pause before the next crash. His eyes closed and his mind raced so fast he couldn't slow it down to focus on any one thing. Blake liked to box breathe. David gave it a shot, then quickly became frustrated when his thoughts pulled him from his breathing after his first three count.

Doctor Kurov materialized sitting on a leather sofa across from him before leaping to her feet and staring at David with icy eyes so different from the eyes he'd seen holding those girls. Realizing she wasn't in a locked cell, she turned and marched into the blackness, her hands wide and searching. David waited for the Genesis to walk her straight back to him from the opposite side.

"What the fuck is this?" she said as she sauntered to him, stopping directly in front of him. He had to crane his neck to look her in the eye or he'd be staring at her breasts.

"You're dreaming," he said.

She pinched herself. "No I'm not. That hurt."

"We're helping you sleep deeply. That won't work here."

"Here? Where is here?" She paced the length of the sofa a few times. "This feels real. Really real. Where am I?"

"You're still in your cell. The same sergeant is standing at the door, making sure you're safe. Why don't you sit down?"

She wiped her red face with her sleeve to absorb the sweat. The Genesis didn't hold back on the details. "Are you actually here? The same guy I saw earlier today? David? Or is this part of the dream?"

David waited for her to take the hint and sit down. When she sat, he leaned forward in his chair. "What happened in that building?"

Her face paled. "What building?"

"Your dream. The children you held. Who were they?"

Her lips parted in shock. The moment she understood the truth of her situation, a mask fell over her face and she closed off like a vault sealing tight.

"You cared about them," he said. "The way you held them in your arms. You pulled them close. What happened? Was it your own explosive?"

Those wide eyes filled with unexpected tears. A few tears escaped down her cheeks, perhaps rattled from the traumatic dream. Whatever was going on in her mind didn't change the bitter way she stared at him.

He waited a minute for her to respond. Another minute. With Blake monitoring the session, he'd know to get to work on researching bombings in a foreign country with reports of innocent civilians being killed. *If the government didn't cover it up.* But the truth would come much faster if he could get her to open up to him.

David touched the space on his shirt where his locket hung, finding nothing in the emptiness of the Genesis coding. Doctor Kurov had faced everything in her interrogations except honest empathy. "I lost someone close to me," he said. "A long time ago. I was so consumed with anger I acted out violently. For a long time, I lost myself." He lowered the top corner of his shirt. The Genesis had recreated the scar on his shoulder.

She squinted as if deciding whether she believed him. "Who?"

"My sister."

"What happened to her?" She leaned forward.

"You first. What happened to those kids?"

She leaned back again and crossed her arms. "They died. Your sister?"

"She died."

Doctor Kurov snorted, a slight smile at the edge of her lips. "A drone strike killed them."

Now he was getting somewhere. He tempered his emotions so as not to seem too desperate for more. "A military drone strike?"

"What happened to your sister?" Doctor Kurov asked. Her shoulders dropped slightly, as if a burden had shifted.

David closed his eyes and saw Laura hanging there, her favorite yellow sundress rippling in the breeze from her bedroom window, the extension cord—the same one she'd used to rig up lights for their late-night study sessions—now twisted around her neck, the ceiling fan motionless above her. He'd desperately tried to lift her by her legs, to release the tension the cord had on her neck. He'd screamed for help and his mother raced in, a face full of abject horror at what her daughter had done to herself. His mother had frozen. David shouted for her to help. He found out later that Laura had been dead for over thirty minutes. He'd been the last one to see her alive. Laura had told him she didn't want to live anymore. Why hadn't he taken her seriously?

"She committed suicide," he said. Even now, he fought back tears and anger at himself for being too stupid to stay with her, to comfort her, to support her with everything she needed to get through the terrible moments she was living.

"How old was she?"

"Fifteen," he said, forgetting he was the one who should be asking the questions.

"I'm sorry."

"Me too. For those you lost. They were just kids. How did you survive the ceiling caving in?"

She shook her head. "I don't want to talk about it. I think we're done here. Let me out of this..." She looked around the space. "Dream. Nightmare. Let me out."

David pulled up the menu. The exit button seemed to glow brighter than the other buttons, although he knew it didn't. She'd been through a lot already, but without answers, he had to force her into another dream sequence. His mission was clear. He needed the bomb's location and the time it would go off. He couldn't take any chances, even if he wanted to give her a break.

David pressed the darker button. Dream sequence two loaded.

Chapter 5

D avid blinked and found himself in a large room with shelving filled with electronic parts that anyone could use for a bomb, or a microwave. He found Doctor Kurov in front of a computer, glaring at a drone's schematic. Not a typical drone. An UCAV: Unmanned Combat Aerial Vehicle. The label at the top corner read Autonix. He'd never heard of that model type, but that meant little, as he wasn't into drones and didn't follow any of the tech companies. Especially those in development by the military. In the screen's corner, the control interface showed autonomous targeting protocols, complex decision matrices. Below the drone's wings were multiple black missile-shaped objects, each bearing the US flag at the tip of the fin. Not surprisingly, she thought the bomb that killed those kids had come from the US.

If the US had been involved, they would have documented missions with the drone name, a battle damage assessment, target identifications, and more details he wasn't an expert in. It wouldn't take long to identify the mission that resulted in those deaths, if the mission was common knowledge. *But if the military covered it up...*

Doctor Kurov wept as she scrolled down the page, reading details from the drone's user manual. Was she seeking revenge for those kids and their families? Or was there more to it? The research wasn't one a bomb-maker would be conducting. It seemed more like someone studying how the technology worked—like she was trying to understand why it happened.

She leaned back in her chair. A sweater was draped over it. The back of the sweater had the words "Beyond the Binary" written on it.

A creaking noise behind him made them both spin around. A ghostly apparition of the older girl from the bombing stood at the shelf, picking up parts, inspecting them, and returning them without comment.

As if the kid could sense their eyes on her, she turned to face Doctor Kurov. A chunk of the left side of her face was crushed, her left arm was gone, and her leg dangled independently of her torso.

Doctor Kurov's breathing quickened, then labored, like she was having an asthma attack.

This isn't real. It can't be. Her nightmares were creating fictitious events. Genesis should have acted like a digital immune system, identifying and isolating these viral memories from reality, but it hadn't had time.

"I'm sorry," she cried, her hands shaking violently. "I didn't build it for this. It wasn't ready to make those decisions."

He would have called the paramedics if he wasn't in her dream. She was going into shock.

Seven people appeared in the room, gathered in a circle, and spoke in whispers. "We're fighting so no other children die because a computer decided they should." It was difficult to tell if this really happened to her or if the Genesis AI had fucked up the sequence. This could be one of her recurring dreams, but clearly in strange, nonsequential chunks spliced by the Genesis. Like trying to piece together a shattered mirror—each fragment reflected something true, but the cracks between them distorted everything. *This won't be easy.*

David studied the faces of the men and looked for weapons or identifying marks in their hands or on their bodies. None wore recognizable markers. Brands like Lululemon wouldn't narrow the search for these people. They had no weapons he could see. A mix of sex, race, bodyfat, colored clothing, and haircuts. This could be a group from Alcoholics Anonymous for all he knew.

One man turned to face Doctor Kurov. He had a sad smile, filled with regret. "Are you sure you want to do this?" he asked her. "Once you join, you're in. At least for this part."

She nodded enthusiastically, her eyes darting to the space where the girl had been a moment ago. Was the kid haunting her mind in real life, too?

"We're happy to welcome you to the guild."

David swallowed hard. *Guild. These are the people that built the bomb.* So many answers hovered right in front of him, and he couldn't do a damn thing to get them, only watch. Modifying the dream wouldn't help.

"Thank you." She didn't smile. If it was an honor, she didn't look like she thought it was. It was her duty. Vengeance for what had happened to those kids. But he still couldn't discern the link or the target for the bomb.

The dead girl stood with her hands to her side, a twisted smile on her face, like she approved of Doctor Kurov's choice. If the others noticed the girl, they made no move to acknowledge her. Doctor Kurov walked to the group, and her own grin looked as real as one of the guy's pink and purple hair streaks.

"Welcome to the Prometheus Guild," Pink Hair said and stepped forward with his arms splayed out wide enough to hug three people.

She nodded, her smile tight and practiced, as if she were only playing the part. There was a flicker of uncertainty, but it was quickly masked. If she had doubted being with these people, why hadn't she walked away? After all the torture she'd endured, how had they not broken her? Soldiers could handle torture for a while, and sometimes those who'd been badly abused or grown up under harsh circumstances. But her? Growing up in a blue-collar home, becoming a doctor—how had she survived?

A guy wearing a blue Kiton suit standing amongst the group of Prometheus members turned sharply, and the side of his head and ear flapped out like the wing of a bird. *He's dead.* Were they all dead? David felt like he had entered an episode of the X-files. He'd never been in a dream that had so many fictitious elements. There was a reason the Genesis logged dreams over an extended time. Still, he had the name Prometheus Guild, and the guild had the bomb.

Doctor Kurov glanced at the dead girl and nodded.

***

David sat in the same chair with Doctor Kurov seated opposite him on the sofa.

Her eyes narrowed, and she snarled. He wondered if he'd lost his connection with her by forcing her back into a dream.

"Anything you want to tell me?" he said.

"Fuck you."

"What is the Prometheus Guild?"

"I want you to let me out of here. Now. You can't keep me in here. This can't be legal." She rubbed the leather on the sofa. *A genie isn't coming out of there.*

"You're dreaming, Lena," David said. "This is all you."

She leaped to her feet, fists clenched tightly, and swung at him. The first punch connected; her assault was so unexpected he hadn't prepared himself. Machine or not, the punch hurt. He shoved the chair back to avoid the second and third swing. Doctor Kurov chased after him, changing to an open palm slap, probably because it was faster and easier to connect.

"Calm down." David bolted off the chair, knocking her down like a defensive end tackling the quarterback on a passing play. She gasped, breathing too spastically to draw in air. "Calm down." He held her hands above her head, waiting until the frantic struggles ceased. The air around her was thick with overheated sweat, clothes damp and skin glistening.

"They're using you," she said after she calmed. "Just like they used me. They'll take all your work and use it to hurt people."

David nodded. "I know." Old news. They'd already gone down that road.

"Then why are you doing this for them? Let me go. Please." Her words were desperate, like a woman stuck in a closet realizing she was claustrophobic.

"Few things are black and white. They're more like sliding scales. What I do for people outweighs some of the damage it's caused. It's better to have good people looking over it than to walk away and let bad people do as they please."

She struggled. "Or destroy it. And nobody has to get hurt. Find another way."

Destroy it. Her solution to the pain she felt from whatever happened to her. *They'd just rebuild.* So, the bomb was real, and she was part of the group that built it. He still had two unanswered questions.

"Where is the bomb?" He relaxed his hold on her, hoping she'd stay calm. "How much time is there before it goes off?"

She sneered. "Tougher men than you have asked me. They didn't get shit either. Fuck you. Fuck whatever this is. All you types are going to hell."

He'd lost her. If she saw him as anything other than an obstacle in her path, maybe he would have broken through. He still believed getting the answers from her directly would be the quickest way.

"I saw you with the Prometheus Guild," he said and leaned back, releasing her hands and getting to his feet.

Doctor Kurov rubbed her wrists. The icy stare he'd seen when he met her was back. "You can't stop it."

"Why don't you tell me what it's about? Why is the Prometheus Guild going to murder innocent people? To teach us all a lesson? So what's the lesson? Those kids that died, it's all about them, right? That Autonix drone that attacked? It's US military. Is that who you're going after? A military base? An office space? They killed the children you loved and you want them to die for it."

"It's so much bigger than that," she whispered.

"Bigger than attacking a military compound?"

She closed her eyes and shook her head. When she opened them, tears had built up again. "They let a machine decide those kids deserved to die. I didn't build it for that. Now let me go." Her lips pressed closed.

For several more minutes, David tried to get her to open up about her relationship with the children. Her lips never parted.

Chapter 6

Light boomed into existence, blinding David as the Genesis lid lifted. He threw his legs over the side and rubbed his head, which was pounding from too many hours in the machine. He couldn't wait for the update that killed that side effect.

Blake stood in front of him, his beard well beyond military regulation thickness, his eyes narrowed and hawk-ish.

"I needed a break," he said.

"Looks like you both did. She stalled out."

"Get all the information? The Prometheus Guild? The bombing? Good places to look for answers." David rubbed his legs to get the blood flowing back to them, not wanting to deal with the pins and needles that sometimes followed the Genesis's movement restrictions.

"Already sent Isaac to do research. He was on a lunch break. As if we need lunch breaks around here." Blake smirked and waited as David threw on his clothes and headed for their office. They stopped for two dark roast, extra old coffees. When they arrived at the office, David dropped into his chair and wheeled toward his desk, reminded of how Doctor Kurov lashed out at him and that look...How many hours of practice had she put into that icy stare of hers?

Isaac's elbow rested on the surface of David's desk as he peeked over. "You okay, tough guy? You look a little lost in thought." Isaac had his conspiratorial face on.

David frowned. "We don't have time for this. Blake texted you a few photos from Genesis with the faces of the Prometheus Guild. Run them through the usual databases. Someone should have intel on them. If the bomb isn't in place, it's one of them that's delivering it."

"Time for what?" He leaned back in his chair and interlaced his fingers behind his head. "You look a little emotional. The doc is a real looker. Wife swap might not be a bad idea. I know I thought about it the moment I saw her picture. Goddamn, and she withstood an interrogation. She can go a few rounds, huh?"

"What did you find out?" Blake stepped up to Isaac. "Sergeant Martin? What did you find out about the Prometheus Guild? The drone?"

"In all of twenty minutes since I heard about it? The drone is standard military tech. There are a dozen of them out on missions right now. I did a few searches of missions involving strikes on misidentified targets, but came up blank. Not to say it isn't out there; I just have to dig more. Access to missions that killed innocent people are going to be highly classified, beyond our scope." Isaac rubbed sweat from his bald head and wiped it on his uniform.

David didn't like Isaac much, but he was a good operator. It took a certain kind of person to work in the Genesis. No different from making it to special operations. They were built different. Sergeant Martin, Isaac, saw some of the worst cases with Genesis. Blake was assigned the higher ranks and David dealt with soldiers that had the most promise to return to active duty. Although David outranked all of them, it was only because of his education. He'd studied nightmares and aiding individuals with post-traumatic stress since university. Isaac certainly didn't view him as a superior with all his combat experience and the death toll he often left in his wake.

"Prometheus Guild?" David stood and wedged his way between Blake and Isaac, feeling the need to be seen as the team lead.

"Check the web. They have a website and they're not afraid to show how pissed off they are about AI research and development. They think we're headed toward Skynet shit—terminators doing their own thinking and killing us off. Called it autonomous, super-intelligent AI systems. Computers making high-level decisions. They don't like it." He smacked the side of the computer. "No worries about these computers. They're so damn old I'm surprised they have Windows."

"Did you check out forums? Message boards?" David asked, his attention drifting to two people he'd never seen before walking past his office toward the boardroom. "Any idea of a target? Someone they blame the most?"

"Twenty minutes, *Captain*. That's all the time I've had," Isaac shrugged. "They hate AI. Shit, AI is in everything. Can't have a phone in your pocket without AI making decisions for you. It probably knows how my ball-sack smells."

"Your phone is always listening. How have you liked the Dove ads? Might help with that." Blake swiped for Isaac's crotch. Isaac stepped back and blocked the movement, somehow having known it was coming. "Don't worry, they have instructions on how to rub on the back of the bottle—no masturbation required."

General Korhonen quick marched into the room, his face unreadable. "Where are we at? What do you know? FBI wants her and they're pushing the Secretary of Defense to step in." He halted in front of David, close enough for David to smell the spearmint gum on his breath and practically taste the mint. He realized he had a hand in his pocket and took it out to stand straighter.

"Sir, we're close. She's definitely assisting with the bomb. She blames the US military on a drone strike gone wrong that killed innocent children. Presumably children under her care. She's not talking, so we don't know who the target is or when the bomb might go off." He rubbed his hands on the side of his pants. "She's working with a group called the Prometheus Guild. They hate artificial intelligence and believe humanity is going to make itself obsolete if something isn't done. I expect the bomb is being used to attack a military base. Likely one working with drones. There's a lot more to follow up on, sir."

General Korhonen smiled. "Come with me, Captain."

David followed General Korhonen out of the room. "Get back to working on those leads," he said to Blake and Isaac as he went out of sight.

"FBI has two agents cleared to be here to relay updates to their team and hit any targets when we have something. They're analysts, so they want hard data." General Korhonen led him to the smaller boardroom, ignoring pleasantries from staff as he passed. He blasted through the door so hard it swung and hit the wall. David imagined the drywall disintegrating on the floor. He didn't bother to check, or it might ruin the dramatic effect of their entrance to the wide-eyed FBI analysts.

"This is Captain Guarnere," General Korhonen said. "He's the team lead on this mission and he's already got more information in a few hours than anyone else has gotten in two days." The general didn't have much of a chest, but he puffed what he could. David would have preferred a more tactical approach to telling the FBI they had intel—something that didn't involve slapping them in the face.

The two analysts tightened their mouths in unison—the official FBI response. David put out his hand to shake theirs. Both leaned away, their eyes finding the table like they hadn't noticed his gesture.

The general had earned them that animosity. When enough time passed for the awkwardness to morph into an elephant in the room, one agent said, "What do you know?"

David briefed them on everything he'd told General Korhonen. The agents immediately went to their laptops and clacked away at their own research. It didn't hurt to have more eyes on. David had done enough to get the credit if they found the bomb and still some credit if they didn't.

While they did so, General Korhonen pulled David out of the room and into a corner at the end of the hallway, his voice low and his hand over his mouth as if he was a hockey coach preventing any cameras from reading his lips. "Tomorrow morning I want you back in the Genesis. There has to be more. I got word the Secretary is going to make us hand her over tomorrow if we don't get answers. Push her. Whatever it takes."

***

"Daddy, why are you still working? I thought we were all on vacation?" Lenny said vacation like cacation, his big brown eyes brimming with tears. David liked to assume it was because he missed him so much, and maybe a little because Lenny had just stubbed his toe on the Thomas the Tank table. "You were gone all day. It's Sunday," he whimpered. David held back a smile because he heard funday not Sunday. The pain in Lenny's toe must have become unbearable, setting off an emotional ride they would take together.

"An important mission came up. Sorry, buddy. I have to help people if I can, right? Like Bruce Wayne would leave a party to go be Batman and save Gotham? Or Clark Kent would leave Lois to go be Superman?" David spread his hand and flew it through the air, impersonating Superman on a quest to save people.

"Can't Uncle Blake go be Superman this time?"

David chuckled. Blake was the real-life Superman. If Superman had no superpowers, a temper, and didn't care who he hurt on the way to justice. He supposed if Superman was real, he might behave just like Blake. Somewhere between the boy scout Superman in the movies and the pure evil Homelander.

"We're working together on this, like the Justice League."

Lenny forced a smile, though his expression clearly stated he wasn't happy about it. David heard Sawyer scoff from the hallway. He stomped past the bedroom door, never making eye contact with them.

"Are you coming with us to see the eclipse?" Lenny pronounced it ekwips.

Helen knocked on the door, smiling sadly. She leaned against the door frame with a plate of sliced fruit in her outstretched hand. Lenny ran to the plate, pulled three large strawberries off it, and devoured them in three gushy bites. The pain in his toe seemed all but forgotten.

"One of the universities has some fun kids' activities planned. Clara read about it in the paper. Sophia doesn't want to come, but I think I'll take the boys."

David nodded, only half-listening, his mind partly on Sawyer. Wasn't it normal for parents to get a little wrapped up in work sometimes? Before David and Helen had opened up to each other and fixed their marriage, she detested his job and the secrets he kept from her. That frustration spilled over to Sawyer as he grew up. David had fixed his marriage, but his relationship with Sawyer hadn't recovered.

"That's great. Lenny will love that," David said, implying Sawyer would hate going, but she'd drag him anyway.

Helen pulled David by the hip to press against her. She kissed the lobe of his ear lightly, and he felt chills run down his back.

"Go complete your mission so we can spend the rest of the week together. Maybe get some time alone." She winked.

"I have a few minutes now," David raised his brows.

Chapter 7
Tuesday

David sat in his chair inside the Genesis. Doctor Kurov lay on the floor, her arms and legs splayed like a car accident photo. She hadn't said a word since she'd arrived and he'd kept quiet, waiting for her to speak first. They hadn't left on good terms, but if she could break through the quiet first, they might find neutral ground. As the minutes passed, David checked options on the Genesis menu and added a few lamps on desks to both ends of the couch. Doctor Kurov lifted her head, observed the desks and additional light, and plopped back down, her head hitting the ground with a thud. More minutes passed while he added incense burning on a stick hanging by one end of an incense holder. David smiled. The holder looked like Gandalf, the incense in his mouth like he was smoking it.

"Cute," Doctor Kurov said casually enough to suggest perhaps her attitude toward him was cooling. "Why am I back here, Dreamcatcher? How is it I feel so tired when I'm dreaming? You'd think I'd get a break."

"I'm running out of time to help you." David wheeled closer to hover over her. Dark circles under her eyes made her look like some of the dead from other soldier's nightmares.

He breathed in sandalwood, reminding him of his grandmother's house; her wooden furniture so dated even she called it old. He loved that furniture. The last time he'd sat in it, his sister Laura had argued for the comfy chair—the one that still had an inch of down and feathers, maybe a little horsehair. Doctor Kurov seemed a lot like Laura—hurt, confused, and willing to die. A knot filled his stomach. He needed her to talk so he could stop thinking.

"Why are you looking at me like that?" Her face softened, like she knew he was scared for her and she felt the weight of it too. "I can't tell you anything. Those in power are never going to change if something big enough doesn't make them change. People need to know. It has to be big."

She was right. It would take something big and public, but it didn't have to involve killing people. Operation Mindwarp had caused so many deaths and the military not only held nobody accountable, they covered it up. "They're going to keep hurting you," he said.

"Not if you stop them." She sat up. "You can stop them from hurting me."

From a civilian's perspective, he understood she might think a soldier in the military in a top-secret project could do something at the highest levels of government. To the FBI, though, he was a jarhead who had to follow orders and stand down when they told him to. "My involvement in this mission ends when you don't talk."

"You already know things. From my dreams. I know you do. So why don't you tell them that?" Despite the desperation and the pleading in her voice, her eyes were dry—she'd already cried all the tears she'd had to cry.

"I don't have a location and I don't have a time. They aren't willing to risk waiting any longer." He took a deep breath, feeling a little overwhelmed. He wanted to help her. "This dream sequence is our last chance. If I don't have answers when I leave the machine, you won't see me again." He paused, ensuring he didn't take his eyes off her. "Or you can just tell me. Give me something. Let me save some lives."

"American lives. So you can go bomb others."

"Why did the drone missile hit that home? What was the target?"

Her lower lip quivered. "Why don't you tell me? Whose decision was it?"

"I don't know."

She growled. "Of course you don't. You're looking for our bomb, not yours. Is a good person who looks the other way when he knows evil is being done behind him still a good person?" she asked. "Is he forgiven of the crime because he can't see? Turning the other cheek was meant to break cycles of violence, not to give you a free pass to ignore them."

The sandalwood had become so thick in the air David coughed, his lungs burning. "I never claimed to be a good person." His voice was raspy and strained.

"You think you are." She pulled him close, the heat of her breath blowing against his neck. Her hands shook just enough to let him know she was terrified. "I don't want to go into my dreams anymore. Please don't."

He pulled away. "I try to help as many people as I can. One day, a soldier might not have to relive the worst moments of their life, like my sister relived every day until she killed herself," he said. If he thought he had an alternative to opening up to her, he would have taken it. Doctor Kurov and Laura were in the same pain; they'd both had someone take something from them they cared about very much. Laura had stopped fighting. Doctor Kurov was only getting started. They both needed someone.

"What happened to her?"

David felt the space on his chest where the amulet should have been. *Keep dancing. Why didn't you keep dancing?* "She was raped when she was fourteen. Found out she was pregnant a few months later. She couldn't take it."

Doctor Kurov's eyes softened a little. "I'm sorry," she said.

"Who were those kids?"

"A close friend of mine's children. Only their mother lived because she was out getting groceries while I watched them. If I hadn't let them run off to see their dad...If I hadn't been in that corner...I'd be dead, too."

"And you blame the government for it."

Tears streamed down her eyes, rushing to the floor. "AIDA," she said.

"What's that? I don't understand."

"My former place of work. We designed the intelligence that killed those kids," she exhaled sharply between breaths.

"AIDA is involved with drones?" David couldn't help leaning in closer to her. "I thought they were a software company."

"Artificial Intelligence and Defense Applications." The words came out like broken glass. "We wrote the programs that saw movement in a family's living room and mistook cooking pots for bomb components. The AI flagged a father making dinner with his children as a chemical weapons operation. Goddamn machine probably filed it away as another 'successful elimination of an imminent threat' in their technical reports. We knew it wasn't ready for this kind of implementation, but they went ahead with it anyway." Doctor Kurov's nails dug into her palms.

David kept still, letting her get it out, hoping she had more to say about the time and location. AIDA was built on government property and mixed with several other agencies in multiple buildings, like a campus.

"Where is the bomb, Lena?"

Her hands quivered. She bit her lip so hard David thought it might bleed. Then her shoulders slouched. "Building C. Where I worked."

"When is the bomb going off?" David asked.

"What day is it?" She sat up and wiped her tears with the backs of her hands and pulled up on the top of her shirt to wipe her nose.

"Tuesday."

She breathed in too deeply, the edge of her lip lifted slightly, and although she did her best to appear indifferent, he could spot a fake stoic. His father had been the real deal, and while mannerisms could be faked, eyes always told the truth. Hers shined with eager anticipation.

"Tomorrow," she said, a brief pause at the beginning of the word, as if she wasn't sure herself.

"Is it with someone? Who is transporting it?"

"Same people in the dream. The Prometheus Guild is going to put themselves on the map with local news agencies. Even if they're caught, people will flock to their cause."

Their cause. Not our cause. That slip told him plenty. Despite helping Prometheus, something felt off—she'd offered that date too easily, probably buying time from Genesis and her nightmares. He wished he could easily conclude that she was a good or bad person, but he was torn."Thank you."

"Can you help me forget?" She grasped David's forearm as he scanned the menu to exit Genesis. He paused with his finger hovering over the exit button.

"Forget?"

"The children. The interrogation. I want to forget it all," she said.

David felt a knot in his stomach. He'd never wanted someone to succeed so badly. She was him, all those years ago, wanting to kick the shit out of the guy that raped his sister. And now he was fighting on behalf of the bully. He hated how it made him feel, and he couldn't do anything about it. Too many innocent people's lives were at stake.

"I'm sorry. I can't. They won't even acknowledge this technology exists." He wanted to tell her he could work with her one-on-one to help her. Maybe treat her privately using the techniques he'd developed before coming to Genesis. Not everyone recovered during his private sessions, but most of them felt better about it. *No.* She'd be going to prison for a long time, and he had Genesis and his family. He couldn't go off on crusades anymore.

"I'm sorry," he repeated and pressed exit.

Chapter 8

David rushed out of the Genesis II, pulling his track pants up and his t-shirt over his head as he rushed for the senior offices and the FBI agents. Blake shouted for him from behind, but he was too focused to listen. He shoved open the door harder than General Korhonen had, hearing a similar slam into the wall. Before he reached the agents and General Korhonen, he said, "I know where the bomb is."

Both agents waved him forward, inviting him to share what he knew. "AIDA. Building C. She's going after the software that guides the drones. She said it's going off tomorrow, but I think she lied. It could be today. Any minute. I think she blames AIDA for allowing their software to be incorporated into the machine when they knew it wasn't ready for military application."

The agents went to their radios and started chattering.

"Proof?" one agent looked up from his computer and asked.

"Her confession," David stated bluntly, a little annoyed at the insinuation in their tone that David might have made it all up. "Are you guys going to investigate the drone that blew up that building?"

Both agents glanced up at him and returned to their computers without answering. *It's a military problem, isn't it?* CID, DOD or maybe JAIC. If they were going to investigate, they would have already. Maybe they hit their intended target after all.

"We'll meet the bomb squad at AIDA," David said.

General Korhonen eyeballed him hard enough to turn him to stone.

"Blake and I are going on site. They might need a negotiator. If Prometheus is there, I can talk them down." *If they won't listen, Blake can handle the rest.*

General Korhonen shook his head. "Not a chance. They have their SWAT teams, qualified negotiators, and bomb guys. You did a great job, Captain. Let them finish up." The general beamed. He patted David on the back so fast David felt like the general expected him to burp.

"Come on," Blake said, motioning David out of the room.

"Excellent work, David," General Korhonen repeated as David left the room. "This is going to open up Genesis to a whole new world of funding."

David followed Blake down the hallway a safe distance until either of them spoke. *Funding. Fucking Funding. The death of those kids is going to give the general more goddamn money. Doctor Kurov's pain is going to pay for the next generation of Genesis.* Seeing General Korhonen smiling made him think of the smug seventeen-year-old that raped his sister and laughed because he'd gotten away with it.

"Let's get going." Blake said twice, snapping him out of his thoughts. "We can be there in time to see it go down."

David pointed at the hallway they'd just come out of. "General Korhonen said—"

"Don't ask permission, David. Take initiative. We don't go in on the assault. We let the initials do their thing. But we can still be there to see it go down. Maybe they'll need our help for something, and we'll offer it." Blake tapped the side of his pants, probably checking for his pocketknife that he relied on like a surgeon's favorite scalpel, then marched to the elevator.

Blake pressed the button. "If anything happens, they'll have a couple of extra pistols on standby. And they'll know who to call the next time they can't get answers out of someone. Maybe we prevent PTSD for some innocent person in the wrong place at the wrong time."

David hadn't thought of that, only the dollar signs in the general's eyes, which made him want to quit his job. Preventing PTSD before it happened? It was possible, though not under their current directorate. *Maybe a Genesis 3.0. Then those kids wouldn't have died for nothing.*

"We aren't dressed for an op," David said. "We're both wearing civilian clothes. Worse, I'm practically wearing PT gear. They'll laugh us off AIDA property."

The elevator pinged before the door closed. Two FBI agents strolled in, each with a suitcase in one hand and a computer bag slung over their shoulders. David and Blake would clear security long before they did and be on the road, driving two hours away to AIDA. David didn't think they'd get there before the FBI, but SWAT would have to clear the perimeter and send in the bomb squad. It would be slow. David could be there to see the bomb being removed from the site and know he'd saved lives. Nobody would ever admit it, and the FBI would take the credit, but Genesis would be the hero in the case.

The elevator chimed. "No time to grab dress uniforms." Blake pushed past three people waiting to go through exit protocols and got in line. He turned and eyed the people he'd passed, daring them to say anything, his smile perfectly passive aggressive. "Let's figure it out when we get there."

***

David had never been on the AIDA campus before. He'd only heard of it through articles in the news and saw pictures occasionally in the paper. As they pulled onto the property, he realized how massive it was. Building beside building, AIDA looked more like a university campus than a tech company. They drove down a road large enough to be a highway, searching for Building C. Each building had a lettered plaque, but they weren't always alphabetical. Building A jumped to Building E because Building B and D were on an adjacent road, maybe built before the others, although the architecture suggested they were all built at the same time. Each building had large one-way looking-glass windows on every floor above the second, and a coffee shop or cafeteria on the bottom floor. The buildings had different foundational colors. A few rose as high as eleven floors.

"That's a lot of space to search," David said as they drove up to a police barricade in front of Building C. *Eleven floors.*

"FBI will figure out exactly where she worked," Blake said, pulling up to a metered parking spot near the police tape. A crowd of employees had gathered at the tape while others were being pulled out of Building C and escorted to the crowd. "Bomb is either on the floor she worked on or in the basement for maximum damage."

The dry heat hit David the moment he stepped out of the car like breaching an incinerator. His pores opened to the sun, releasing beads of sweat down the front of his shirt. They made their way through the crowd to the line. Someone in the crowd was puffing on a cigar, and two others walked past him laughing, unaware that any second they could become chunks splattered on the concrete. Local police hovered at the tape, keeping everyone back. David couldn't see a single FBI jacket.

"We aren't getting past these guys," David said. Unless they stumbled upon someone they knew working the case, they'd watch from the sidelines like everyone else.

Blake ducked under the tape.

"Hey, stop!" Two officers simultaneously shouted at Blake. They rushed over but hesitated to put a hand on him. Instead, their hands went to their tasers. *Better than their guns.*

He showed them his DOD identification and waved for David to follow. "We're working the case with the FBI. Ask the agent in charge. Let them know there are a couple of Genesis guys here. They'll know what that means."

The female officer clicked on her radio. "Dispatch, I have two men from the DOD claiming to be part of the investigation. They say they're with Genesis and want to talk to the officer in charge." She shook her head, releasing the button on her radio and stepping up to Blake to look him in the eye. She was only a few inches shorter than him. "If you're wasting my time, I'm throwing you in the cruiser."

"Yes, ma'am," Blake smiled, giving her a two-finger salute.

Seven minutes later, two men approached, their expensive suits matched only by their disdainful frowns. "You're the two that caused all this?" the agent asked.

David saw Blake's bravado fade a little with the agent's tone. "Finding the target? Yeah."

"Goddamn waste of resources," the other agent said, his hands pressed tightly into his hips. "Don't know what the hell they involved you two for. Above my paygrade. Goddamn waste of resources. Come on. Might as well let you heroes see the work that goes into things when you run your mouths."

The agent led them to a semi-truck with a large box on its back, parked between two buildings, which shielded it from the street and any media cameras. 'FBI' was written on the side. *Hiding their logo? Not like them.*

The agent in charge introduced himself as Special Agent Cameron. They shook hands as a formality. David could feel the heat radiating off Cameron, and it wasn't just because it was so damn hot out.

"We didn't find shit in there. Again. We already had a team come here yesterday, so the CEO came down to talk to me about twenty minutes ago to ask if we're planning to keep coming back. Most of his staff suddenly went home sick, and I bet everybody calls in sick for a few days. Building is clear," Cameron said. "If it was going off today, it's not here."

Did I get the day wrong? Was she serious about it being tomorrow? David couldn't believe he'd misread her signals. His mouth hung open, but he couldn't think of what he wanted to say. Finally, he said, "Maybe it's on the way here. Should we clear everyone out and set a trap?"

"Goddamnit, do you know how much time we wasted here? Hours we don't have. We've scared a lot of people. The hotline is going to go nuts when someone's spotted carrying a gym bag." Cameron's hand shook like he wanted to punch something, but he held himself back.

Being on site didn't feel as good as David had imagined.

"Maybe she sent us to the wrong building?" Blake asked. "What other buildings could be her target?"

Cameron fumed as they entered the trailer. "We already sent teams to search the rest of the buildings for any suspicious packages. Nothing. We're clearing out of here. I'll leave a team to monitor activity, working with AIDA security, because my superiors want to play it safe, but I don't expect shit to happen. There goes my damn budget. Someone has to make that girl talk."

The trailer was much larger inside than David expected. Nothing like television suggested. Computer after computer lined one side of the wall, many with agents seated in them. A few seats were strapped in, probably for transport. The back of the trailer, near the driver, was a lounge area with leather chairs set up like two aisles in an airplane, only facing each other. Hooks with gear bags were bolted to a shelf.

"I think you already tried that tactic," Blake said, admiring the scope of the operation and then turning to leave. They had nothing to gain with the FBI. "We saw the results."

David wondered how much she'd have to suffer before she gave up intel. Probably a lot more than they had time for before the bomb went off. If anything, their cruelty would strengthen her resolve to show the world how dangerous men can be when they think they're in the right. *Hell, is she wrong?* If the bomb went off, the world would discover how dangerous AI could be when left to make decisions on its own. A machine had killed children because everyone thought someone else would make sure it made the right decisions. Maybe that made all of them responsible—AIDA, the military, everyone involved.

"Do you see all these experts at work here?" Agent Cameron said. "The agents in the video feeds over there. Thousands of man hours in this, and nothing to show for it. Not so much as a hint that anyone other than Doctor Kurov was interested in this place."

"Impressive," David said, at a loss for words. What was Agent Cameron expecting? An apology for doing his job? One camera displayed the office he remembered from her dream. He made a mental note of the caption at the bottom that read 803.

David followed Blake out of the trailer, the outside air even hotter thanks to the few minutes they'd spent in the chilly command center.

"Should we head back to Genesis?" David asked. Before Blake could answer, David said, "Let's look around. If they're clearing the site, they won't mind us checking out her office. Maybe we'll find some personal effects that will tell us more. Come on, let's jet."

"Charlie Mike."

Doctor Kurov worked on the eighth floor—803. The FBI still had the elevators out of service, so David led the way up the stairs. The first three floors zoomed by, the adrenaline not slowing until the fourth floor. David preferred hitting the weights to doing cardio and clearly his functional weight training hadn't paid off. Each step felt like he had bricks instead of quads and his lungs burned like they had during his Genesis basic training bootcamp. He certainly didn't feel like he could hit a mile in under seven minutes like he had then.

When they reached the eighth floor and lugged into room three, a scan of the place confirmed it was the same as Doctor Kurov's nightmare. The computer desk and chair were in the same spot. A lot of the materials David had assumed were for making a bomb still lingered on the shelves, a layer of dust covering them, unlike her nightmare, where everything looked clean. Her Beyond the Binary sweater was still draped on her chair, so maybe it hadn't been that long since she met with the Prometheus Guild.

Three FBI agents eyed them suspiciously, asked for their identification, and left shortly after David explained what they were there for.

"This room," David said, turning in a slow circle. Reality and memory merged until he wasn't sure which version he was standing in. "She met the Prometheus Guild here."

Blake lifted papers off her desk and scanned them, tossing them aside as he concluded they weren't relevant. He moved the mouse that was on her desk. When nothing happened on the monitor, he followed the cord to the back of the desk and down to a cupboard. The computer was gone. "FBI took it?"

"Good chance. Or she did. Out of our reach either way. They aren't going to cooperate anymore, not after this." David rifled through papers on an adjacent desk, knowing she was too smart to leave plans for her bomb on it, and the FBI would have already rummaged through it for anything valuable. "This is a dead end. We need to go back to Genesis."

"She got me too," Blake said, patting David's shoulder as he walked by. "I thought her breakdown was the end, but she played her part well. Can't imagine why she'd want to visit with the FBI, though. They're getting desperate and that's bad for her."

"The room is exactly the same as her nightmare. Only some additional dirt." David ignored Blake's consolations. He ran his finger along the shelf with boxes of wires in them. His finger returned covered in a small layer of dust. "That means she hasn't been back here, and no cleaners have been in."

They tossed the two garbage cans they found in the room. One had a broken pair of 3D glasses, crumpled papers with articles on AI breakthroughs—all old news. Blake used a pen to stir up the half-eaten Chinese take-out, as if he might find a fortune cookie hidden inside that would tell them everything. The more he stirred, the more David wanted to gag at the smell of rancid fish and sweet, sickly chicken balls.

"FBI wasn't interested in this? I don't suppose anyone is checking the Panda Express for the bomb?" Blake chuckled. "The smell is bad enough for me to want to toss a grenade into this room."

David didn't think Blake minded the smell at all.

Car horns blared outside. David peeked out the window to watch the FBI parade leave the campus. *How could I be so wrong?* He was good at reading people. It's what he did. How could he help clients resolve their emotional trauma if he couldn't even read them?

"Let's jet," David said. "I don't think there's anything here. The FBI cleared it out."

"You want to get some Chinese food on the way back?" Blake asked.

Chapter 9

David drove with the car window down, trying to air out the smell of coffee and sandwiches he and Blake had consumed on the drive back. He kept replaying Doctor Kurov's words in his mind, trying to understand where he'd gone wrong. She'd been so certain about AIDA, almost too certain. Like she needed him to look there instead of...somewhere else. What else had she said? What had he missed?

He gave Helen a quick call to let her know he'd be working late and not to worry. Lenny insisted on saying hello, then told him everything he'd missed that day. Cute at first, then David felt guilty that he'd somehow skipped the best vacation ever.

"Why aren't you home?" Lenny had asked after he'd run out of things to talk about, including his lightning speed devouring of *two* grilled cheese and bacon sandwiches. David imagined he meant two halves, but didn't ask.

"Two sandwiches? Both had cheese *and* bacon? And you ate it *all*?" He pretended to struggle to catch his breath. "I'll be home before you know it. Stuck at work trying to make the world a little safer."

"Just put out the Bat-Signal, Daddy. Batman can help. Then you'll be home earlier," Lenny said with all the innocence and earnest of a six-year-old.

"I'll see what I can do. I haven't spoken to Commissioner Gordon in a while."

"He'll help, Daddy. He always does."

"Goodbye buddy, I'll see you later," David said, one hand on the steering wheel, the other aiming for the end button on his cell.

"He doesn't think we need the Justice League?" Blake asked.

"Batman would do exactly what the FBI is trying to do: torture the information out of her. I don't think he'd be a lot of help."

They headed through security with the enthusiasm of two men who felt too old to stand in front of General Korhonen and get word-vomited on. Blake and David hadn't reached the elevators before running into the general.

"You fucked up this mission badly," General Korhonen vomited, not bothering to keep his voice lowered despite all the people at their desks on both sides of them. The general wasn't known for his patience or tact for discipline. David hadn't experienced it before, but now that he had, he could see the reputation was warranted.

"Sir, there was no way to be completely certain."

"No shit you weren't certain. You sounded certain, until just now. And you pissed off the FBI, wasting hours of their time on that goose chase. Your report better be damn good, Captain. If you sent them there on a hunch and didn't have hard evidence..." The general's face had turned so many shades of red, he could have been in a cartoon.

"Are you okay, sir?" David asked.

"Am I okay? Do I look okay, Captain? Huh?" General Korhonen stepped up into David's face, the Brut aftershave wafting off his skin.

"No, sir. You don't."

"You're off the damn case, Captain." He threw up his arms. "Thanks to you, there is no goddamn case. We could have done so much with this project if you hadn't fucked this up. I put you in charge because I didn't want a hardass like Master Chief pissing all over it. Clearly a mistake."

David noticed more than a few people in their cubicles had either put headphones on or headed to the watercooler to give them some privacy. "Sir, anyone could have made a judgement error on this. She confessed. Should we not have taken her word on it? We only catalogued her nightmare for—"

"Excuses? You're running your mouth with excuses? At least when this guy fucks a mission, he makes sure there's nobody left to talk about it." General Korhonen pointed a thick finger at Blake, then addressed him. "So what the hell happened to you? Why didn't you stop him from making an ass out of all of us?"

David stepped in before Blake could. This was his mess, and he was in charge. "I'm sorry, sir. We—"

Blake's eyes narrowed, and he spoke through clenched teeth. "I'm looking at the only ass in the room, respectfully, sir."

David didn't think the general had any darker shades of red left in him, but Blake proved him wrong.

"Consider yourself on leave for insubordination, Master Chief." General Korhonen's tone quieted, like the calm before a storm. "I don't want to see either of you the rest of the week. Unpaid leave." He said unpaid with an edge he clearly wanted to stab them with.

The room had become eerily silent until the elevator pinged and four FBI agents hauled Doctor Kurov toward the security exit. Two of the agents were the same two from the general's office. General Korhonen turned to watch them leave, and David could practically see him tallying his financial losses.

The agents took a detour around the desks to get close to David and the general before heading to security. It was a slap in the face from the FBI, who were probably happy the military brats had failed. Doctor

Kurov's eyes had reverted to the icy stare he'd seen the first time he met her. He'd never gotten her the beer and chicken salad.

As they approached, Doctor Kurov leaped over and grabbed David by his shirt.

"I'm sorry," she said to David as the agents worked to pull her away.

"Easy on the shirt," David said to the agent who was prying her fingers off him.

Blake pushed the agent back and let Doctor Kurov stand close to David. David didn't react. He waited with arms to his sides, indifferent, like she wasn't there pinning herself to him.

David finally let himself look into her eyes, beyond the layers of pain, deep into the person he knew she was. If only things had been different for her. "Murder is always a cycle, filtered through a personal lens. I'm sorry I couldn't stop you. I hope they do."

Doctor Kurov eased her grip and stepped backwards into the fold of agents. "Keep your head up, Dreamcatcher. In a moment as brief as a heartbeat, the world will change."

Her world had already changed in a heartbeat. Whose world was she going to change in that same heartbeat? They all watched as the FBI escorted her out of the building. David shook his head, frustrated at himself for not having gotten through to her. Blake turned to face him the moment she cleared the exit.

"What do you want to do?"

General Korhonen had lost all his energy and now just looked tired. "I don't want to see you two for the rest of the week." With shoulders slouched, the general slunk out of the room like someone had taken his lunch money and he had to go another day without it.

"Go home," David answered after a long pause.

Blake threw an arm around David's shoulder. "Cheer up. Not all missions succeed. This one was set up to fail from the beginning.

Genesis only had a day to collect her nightmares, and even with the AI assist, there's no way that's enough time. We had to rely on a blend of her and the machine. Can't win them all, you know?"

David shrugged. "Sure." There were a lot he hadn't won. A lot of his clients hadn't returned to active duty. General Korhonen had imposed a six-month limit on soldiers returning to combat. Six months was only enough time to check boxes and turn Genesis into a processing plant.

"This mission had to be the one he made me lead?" David looked around for something he could kick. A lot of the faces in the office returned to their desks, most pretending he wasn't standing there. A few gave sympathetic smiles.

"Don't beat yourself up for it."

Any beating he gave himself wouldn't be half as bad as the one Doctor Kurov was going to get. "Why did she lie about it? She knew this would happen."

They headed through security, taking their time getting scanned for anomalies on their way out.

"It happens."

David cringed. Blake always had an answer, but rarely a helpful one. Of course it happened. He wasn't an idiot. "Why was I so stupid and believed her?" he asked, more to himself than to Blake. "Her eyes, her posture...she let go of a burden when she told me, I know it."

Blake snorted. "Don't underestimate a woman's power to manipulate. She knew how to play you, and she did. Got both of us. Come on, let's get a few beers and forget about it."

David paused at the scanner. "This doesn't have to be over. Come on, let's jet to the war room."

Blake crossed his arms. "Going against the big man's orders? I like it." He tapped David on the shoulder as he headed back into the building toward the elevator. "What do you want to do? Get back inside the Genesis? We still have a few secondary nightmares catalogued."

"I think we have everything we need. We just don't know it." David licked his lips and tasted salt. When had he sweat so much?

"We were wrong about the bomb."

"She must have sent us on a goose chase because of how close we were to the truth. What if she knew we had everything we needed, so she panicked?" David rubbed the side of his head with his fingers, pressing deep into his temples, hoping to keep his growing headache at bay. He'd missed his third coffee of the day and his last coffee hadn't been nearly strong enough. He could go for a Ristretto. A small taste of home would do him some good.

"'A moment as brief as a heartbeat,'" David muttered.

"What?" Blake asked.

"Nothing. Just thinking out loud." But the phrase stuck with him, needling at his consciousness like a splinter he couldn't quite reach.

"We should watch her other dreams, even if we can't go interactive with them," Blake said. "She might have worried you were about to stumble onto her best kept secret."

"You follow up with her other dreams. Anything useful Genesis catalogued. I'm going in to re-check what I already saw. Feels like the answer is there. I have it, and she knows it. Something I missed."

"Charlie Mike," Blake said and walked ahead to the Genesis III. David headed for Genesis II. He peeled off his shirt and sat on the bed.

When Blake saw his face, he walked over and sat beside him. "You're doing a great job on this mission. Delegating tasks well. I saw you break through to her, even if she lied to you. Another day or two and she'd be singing without the need for violence. Not the way I would have played it, but I think in this case it was the right way."

"This coming from the guy that believes failure doesn't deserve a reward?"

"Do you know what separates most men during selection? It's not about being the fittest guy or the smartest guy. Certainly not the most aggressive jarhead in the group."

David peered at Blake. "The guy with the most heart?"

Blake punched him in the shoulder. "Snap out of that gooey shit. The guy who doesn't quit, even if it doesn't go well the first time. Having the guts to fail and hurt and get up and do it again because that's what the mission demands, that's what makes a great candidate. I've seen a ton of fit guys go home to their wives with nothing but excuses because they still couldn't face the fact that they quit. Quitters don't make good operators. Fighters do. And you're fighting right now."

"There are a lot of lives on the line."

"There always are. With Genesis, we deal with one life at a time, but we're here because that one life can save a lot of other lives. Putting the best damn leaders back into combat without PTSD is an incredibly powerful thing to do. I think we've saved more lives in our time here than I did as a SEAL and in the Unit combined. Doesn't make the sacrifice any less. Just different."

"Thanks, Blake. Makes me sick to think the bomb could go off any second and the answer is right in our faces."

"Then let's get to work." Blake fist bumped David then headed off to the Genesis III and lay inside.

David inhaled and let out a big breath, the burden of the mission weighing a little less on him. *Let's get back to work.*

He lay back and pressed a button on the screen beside his leg. The lid closed and sealed him in. He sat on his chair, looking at an empty sofa. For a minute, he simply stared at the sofa, playing through the conversation he'd had with Doctor Kurov.

David loaded the first sequence.

Chapter 10

David was in Doctor Kurov's point of view as he watched her dream play out. She rocked in her chair with the two kids in her lap. She whispered something to them, but he couldn't hear. Maybe she'd mumbled a prayer or a familiar sound. Every detail mattered, but this was just before the bombing and Prometheus, so she wouldn't be giving away vital intel. Unless the AI had filtered out an anomaly in the sequences it compiled and inadvertently removed something vital.

The building shook. The kids popped off her lap and headed to the other room, just as they'd done previously. He heard the familiar buzz and waited for the second quake.

The ceiling caved in. Debris kicked up smoke all around. Two feet away, a section of the wall revealed a steel beam. Now he was seeing what the machine hadn't had time to compile last time. She rolled to the beam as the rest of the foundation collapsed, engulfing the room in smoke. Brick rained down, filling most of the empty space. She crawled through a small hole in the wall that must have collapsed when the bomb went off.

So this is how you survived when nobody else did. A lucky break. She should have found God instead of the Prometheus Guild; the odds of making it out of that building were almost none. Someone had watched over her and not so she could become what she had. Fate didn't turn good people into killers. They did that by themselves.

As she stumbled onto the road, people shouted questions, asking if she was okay and what had happened. Her ears rang from the collapse and although she could hear their words, the pinging in her head prevented her from forming a coherent sentence. Bystanders worked together to pull bodies out of the rubble. She watched as a young man carried the body of the little girl that had sat on her lap onto the street and placed her down beside the rest of the dead. Doctor Kurov collapsed and cried. Her eyes shifted upward, as if to plea to God, and David saw a small dark object floating in the air, momentarily uncovered by a passing patch of cloud. That's how she knew what had happened. She saw the drone. But no logo or identifiable feature was visible from that distance, so how she connected it to Autonix was beyond him.

The dream exited. David leaned back in his virtual chair, staring at the empty sofa, replaying every word she'd said to him since they met. *Am I missing something?*

He loaded the next dream sequence.

***

David scanned the drone on Doctor Kurov's computer screen, again seeing the American flag on the tail. Her eyes drifted to the bottom of the screen and paused. A bullet-point listed the drone as having the latest technology, including an AI autonomous system. Wording directly below that said:

Eliminate Human Error. Embrace AI Precision.
In the heat of battle, human judgement falters. Our
cutting-edge AI Combat Autonomous System doesn't.
Powered by advanced algorithms crafted by elite mili-
tary strategists, our autonomous system delivers:

Lightning-fast tactical decisions

Unbiased combat analysis

Continuous adaptation to evolving threats

Upgrade your military operations with the future of
warfare technology.

The Autonix Combat Drone: Where AI meets military
might.

She scrolled past the technical specifications: neural networks trained on thousands of combat scenarios, decision matrices that could process threat assessments in milliseconds, computer vision systems that claimed to distinguish combatants from civilians with 98% accuracy. All the confidence of mathematics applied to the messiness of human conflict.

The Genesis AI hadn't compiled this part of her dream the last time David had been in it. He recalled what Kurov had cried: *I didn't build it for this. It wasn't ready to make those decisions.* If she had something to do with the drone programming, it made sense that she wanted to destroy it.

Through her peripherals, he scanned for a website address. The file wasn't online. It was a PDF. She'd found it on her work drive. Probably classified, but she'd have access because she was a researcher. That's why Isaac hadn't found it. But none of this ruled out AIDA as the most likely target with Autonix being manufactured on a military base, which made it nearly impossible to hit.

Doctor Kurov turned to see the girl with her face hanging open. David studied the scene, replaying his memory of what he found in her office with what he saw now.

Nothing. There's nothing. He skimmed the room twice more, following her vision. He saw a pair of 3D glasses on the table. He'd seen those before—crushed and in the trash. Now, the glasses were in perfect condition, resting in the middle of her desk like she'd used them recently. Several of the papers that he'd seen in the trash were beneath the glasses, like she'd walked by and swiped it all off the desk.

What good would 3D glasses be? What was she watching with them? Her gaze returned to the computer, and she pressed two buttons to put it to sleep.

As she walked across the room to stand next to members of the Prometheus Guild, he inspected the papers on the desk beneath the glasses and saw nothing that required them—no anaglyphic papers.

He desperately wanted to explore the rest of the room, but without Doctor Kurov, he was like a puppet whose strings only moved in preset patterns. The Genesis menu offered no freedom to pause or explore.

Doctor Kurov finished her indoctrination into the Prometheus Guild and the dream ended.

David sat in the same virtual chair, so uncomfortable he leaped to his feet and kicked the chair into the dark void.

Her job is in AI research. If I assume she programmed the AI system that led to the strike, her target has to be the drone tech itself, or the office she built it in. I know it's not in her office, and even if it was, the FBI are still watching it. What does that leave? If she didn't know the purpose of her programming, she might blame the person that weaponized her research, but a bomb would be overkill for any one person.

David exited the Genesis and immediately sought Blake, who'd already left Genesis III. He found Blake in their office, running online searches.

"Find anything?" David asked.

Blake shook his head. "Nothing. A couple of meetups with Prometheus. She seemed a little tense in the dream, not like she was when she met them. But nothing much came of it. If there's something to gain, we haven't catalogued it yet. How did you do?"

"Need some coffee. You?" If he could have, he might have curled up into a ball on the floor and slept.

Blake shrugged, stretched, and followed David to the lounge. David was about to say the only thing he found in her dream was a pair of 3D glasses, when he noticed a female staff member seated at the chair wearing a sweater that said "Beyond the Binary" on it. "What the hell?" David said, much louder than he meant to.

Blake and the woman in the chair spun to look at him. "What?" Blake glanced at the woman, did a quick survey of the room, then found David. "What?"

The woman seemed uncomfortable with his gaze and turned back to the table.

"'Beyond the Binary.' That's what was written on Doctor Kurov's sweater," David said, his eyes following the woman as she uncomfortably made her way out of the lounge. He watched her like a security camera following a homeless person in a bank. "The one hanging from her chair. I assumed the AIDA logo was on the front. Did you see her sweater? What logo was that?"

Without waiting for Blake's response, David chased after the woman and caught her as she entered the war room. "Excuse me?" he called to her. "Ma'am? Ma'am!" She stopped and turned. She must have been in her early twenties, with short brown hair pulled over to one side to cover a buzz cut. Her eyes were wide enough to slot a quarter into.

"Yes, sir?" She snapped her heels together and saluted, green enough not to remember she shouldn't salute in civilian attire.

"Your sweater. Is that from AIDA?" David asked.

"AIDA? Sir, sorry sir, I don't know what that is, sir." She seemed to get taller after answering his question, as if there was a position of attention and a position of *really* at attention.

"Where did you get that sweater?"

She glanced down at the words on her sweater like she hadn't noticed them before and wanted to tear them off for being there. "Sir, Bloomington University, sir. Sorry sir, I should not be parading in the war room in these clothes. Sir, permission to change, sir."

"Bloomington University? Beyond the Binary. That's their slogan?" David leaned in, perhaps too close.

"Sir, yes sir," she said, leaning back like a soldier that had stood at attention too long and might pass out.

"Where is Bloomington?"

"Sir, here in California, sir. Maybe an hour away, sir."

"Do you know what 'Beyond the Binary' means?" David asked. Blake pushed up against him, just as eager to hear her answers. Her eyes darted from David to Blake.

"Sir, from what I understand, it references their advances in technology and their inclusivity and forward thinking, sir." She took two steps back. "Sir, can I go now, sir?"

"Do they do AI research? Are they known for their advancement in AI autonomy?"

"Sir, they do AI research, like a lot of universities. I guess that's one thing they're known for, sure."

"That's all, thank you," David said, his mind reeling with implication. "If she had connections to Bloomington, she wouldn't blame them for the Autonix, would she? It doesn't make sense if AIDA developed the technology and the military implemented it into their drone. That's like blaming the drill sergeant for what the soldier did in combat. Unless…"

Blake straightened. "Unless what?"

"Unless Bloomington's research laid the groundwork. The fundamental AI principles that AIDA built upon. In her dream, she was fixated on that autonomous system, but she wasn't just angry at AIDA—she might have been angry at the whole concept." David's eyes narrowed. "What if she traced it back to its academic roots? The theories that made it possible? She might think it's more practical to target the minds that aren't thinking clearly when they teach students the principles, rather than the students themselves."

"And Bloomington would be a lot easier to hit than AIDA's facility. We should tell Korhonen."

David nodded grimly. "Let's hope we're right."

Chapter 11

David spent two hours digging through the internet before he went to Korhonen's office. The university's faculty directory was public, but Doctor Kurov's name didn't appear in any department listings. The engineering department's research page showed several AI initiatives that could have interested Prometheus, but nothing definitive. LinkedIn showed she'd done guest lectures at three universities, but Bloomington wasn't one of them. Still, that BU sweater in her dream had to mean something. If he ignored it any longer, he'd have to live with himself if innocent people died because he didn't act.

They'd left the general's office after updating him on their suspicion, getting all the gratitude of a grunt as he sent them away and promised to call the FBI.

David sat at his desk, finger drumming against the wood, joining Blake in a rendition of Thunderstruck. By now, FBI agents would be searching the engineering labs. David checked his watch and realized he'd missed dinner at home. He was about to call Helen when the office phone rang. The call display said G Korh. David swallowed and lifted the receiver.

"Captain Guarnere," General Korhonen said, his voice so strained David knew what he was going to say before he said it. "You successfully sent the FBI on another useless goose chase. Thankfully, they only sent a few officers and not a goddamn command center. Their background check shows she was never on faculty or enrolled there. The sweater was probably a gift from one of her colleagues."

"Sir, I checked what I could access, but without higher clearance—"

"Fuck. You damn well didn't know her target was Bloomington, did you?"

"Technically no, sir. But the sweater draped over her office chair—"

"You're taking the heat on this one if it comes down the chain. I'm not covering for you. Your job is to find the damn bomb, not point the FBI to every fucking trinket she has in her dream. Goddamnit, Captain. I don't want to hear another word from you. Go home, Captain." Without giving David a chance to speak, the phone went dead.

David lowered the phone, hearing the click as the base cradled it. His face burned hot and he could feel a tightness in his chest. *This isn't what I signed up for.* The lights in the room made a buzzing noise he hadn't noticed before. He kept his hand on the phone, waiting for a follow-up call to tell him they found the bomb after all, and he was very sorry for treating David that way. The call never came.

"David?" Blake whispered.

David closed his eyes and squeezed them as tight as he could. *Wrong again. What's the goddamn target?* He slammed his hand down on the table. Then he did it again. Three more times.

"One of those targets is the right one. It has to be," Blake said. "We just don't have the right day or time. Who else could be the target?"

"The AFRL," David said.

"Who?"

"The Air Force Research Laboratory. It's the most likely place they keep the Autonix." Nothing about her screamed an attack on a military base. Not only due to the abysmal odds of getting a bomb onto the base, but even if they successfully destroyed the building, it wouldn't have nearly the impact on media as thousands of innocent civilians. Soldiers dying didn't hit the same, even if it would be tragic. David didn't think that was her target.

"So one of the three. Let's talk hypothetical. If she was going to get a bomb onto a base, how would she do it?"

Everything we've talked about has been hypothetical. "She didn't even attend Bloomington," David said, wanting to listen to loud music to drown out the voice in his head. "Can you believe that? The sweater probably wasn't hers. It's a shared office, right? I'm not a damn investigator. How would I know?" It was going to be a long week thinking of all the ways General Korhonen was going to take it up with him. He would have preferred the discipline happened right away. But what was Korhonen going to do? Fire him? He did exactly what was asked of him.

"Focus up," Blake snapped. "Stop feeling sorry for yourself. Assholes like General Korhonen are everywhere. It's not our job to make that dick happy so he can bathe in money. It's our job to find the bomb, and you're in charge. So act like it."

"The FBI won't back us up anymore. We're on our own."

"Then let's jet," Blake said in a mocking tone. "Being solo behind enemy lines is nothing new. It's where I'm the most comfortable. So get comfortable and let's figure this thing out because there are shit tons of people counting on us." Blake took a tight grip on David's shoulder. "We have three possible targets. Any reason to believe there might be a fourth?"

"In this case, sure. She might target someone who shared her research. Or whoever implemented it into the Autonix."

Blake sipped his coffee and sputtered it up. "David, you need clear thinking on this. Take a minute. No way she's going after something small. If that was the case, the FBI would have found a pistol, not a bomb kit. And Prometheus will want to pack a punch."

David wanted to punch him for his condescending tone, even if he was right. He turned and faced the door to avoid eye contact. "If she's working with the Prometheus Guild, the target has to align with their objectives, too. That's what we're missing. We're focused solely on her. What about them? Does the FBI have any of them in custody?"

Blake smiled, picked up the phone, ran through a list of recently called, and found whatever he was looking for. He hit the speaker button when it dialed. A male FBI agent answered.

"I need to speak to Special Agent Cameron, working the bomb case."

"Can I ask who's calling?" the voice on the phone said.

Blake hesitated. "General Korhonen," he said.

David threw up his hands and slapped the mute button. "What the hell are you doing?" he whispered.

Blake put up a single finger.

One minute? For what?

"Special Agent Cameron," came a tight-lipped voice from the other end of the line.

"Hello Special Agent Cameron, this is Master Chief Powell," Blake said.

"I was told General Korhonen was on the line." Agent Cameron sounded more bored than angry. "I'm not in the military, but I assume impersonating a superior officer is a hefty offense. What do you want, Master Chief? Hopefully not to send us to another dead end?"

"You know as well as I do how this works. Everything is a shot in the dark. How many sites have you hit today and been wrong,

Agent?" Blake glanced up at David. "By the way, you're on speaker with Captain Guarnere."

"Pleasure," Agent Cameron said. "We've visited a few."

"Guessing you haven't found the bomb yet?"

"Get to the point, Master Chief. Two days of dead ends. Clock's ticking, and we're no closer to finding this bomb. I'll give you some leeway, but not much."

"We've been working on the assumption that we can tie Doctor Kurov directly to the bomb's location. But what does your team have on the Prometheus Guild? We should start working together and sharing information, Agent. You have resources and access to information we don't, and we have details from the doctor's nightmares that link her to both Prometheus and the Autonix bombing."

An exhausted snort came through the line. "We're gathering intel on Prometheus right now. It wasn't on our radar. You guys did a good job finding that link at least."

"Do you still have Doctor Kurov in your custody?" David asked.

A heavy breath cracked through the receiver. "She's being transferred to DHS shortly."

"Can you hang on to her? I need to talk to her. I think I can break through."

"Sorry, Captain, I can't withhold the transfer without a damn good reason. It's the end of the day and the DHS is picking her up in the morning. We have another team coming in to speak with her overnight, but they aren't taking visitors. If you want to drive here in the morning, roughly an hour and a half, I'll send you the address. You'd get a quick conversation with her."

"Do you think you'll have more on the Prometheus guild by then?" Blake asked, as if going there was a foregone conclusion.

"Good chance. Our analyst is putting together a report."

"We'll see you in the morning."

"I'll have Agent Chen meet you in reception and bring you up," Agent Cameron said. "Bring whatever intel you have."

"Wilco," Blake said, then gave Agent Cameron his cell number and hung up. "Ready?"

David laughed. "I guess we're going to Quantico tomorrow. Glad you didn't mention our intel is in our brains because Genesis isn't leaving this building."

Chapter 12
Wednesday

B lake picked up David at eight in the morning and talked the entire drive. Although David heard every word, he didn't listen to any of it, too focused on what he would say to Doctor Kurov to get her to open up.

"Let's get a cold beer and chicken salad on the way," David said.

They followed the car's navigation system to the San Diego Field Office. The building was a modern, multi-story structure with a mix of clear glass and light gray concrete, blending in like an informal camouflage with the surrounding office park. Despite its blending, the security guards at the gates made it clear they hadn't stopped at a typical office building.

"Name?" the security guard at the gate asked the moment they pulled up, his hand so far from his pistol David didn't think he could defend himself in time if Blake jumped out at him. *Are these private guards or FBI home grown?*

"Master Chief Blake Powell, Captain David Guarnere, here to see Special Agent Cameron at his invitation," Blake said.

The agent scanned his notepad and waved them through. David couldn't tell if he'd actually found their names. His eyes never paused, only scanned.

They parked in visitor's parking near the front entrance. Inside, security was less impressive than Genesis, consisting only of metal detectors and x-ray machines. They found an Asian woman in a black suit standing near the guest check-in, watching them like a snake on a mouse. David waited for her to pounce as they moved within arm's reach.

"Cap and MC?" Agent Chen greeted. Her hard exterior melted away as her words came out soft and thoughtful. She extended her hand.

"Agent Chen?" David shook her hand, holding the chicken salad and beer in a paper bag in his opposite hand.

"Call me Jia."

Her handshake was surprisingly firm for a fairly petite hand. She might have weighed a hundred and twenty pounds, but he saw a fire in her eyes a lot of people probably underestimated. Jia led them to the elevator and up to the seventh floor, where they shook hands with Agent Cameron who escorted them to a boardroom.

"Where are your things?" he asked. "Copies of your files? Reports?" He had a file cupped in his hand and pressed tight to his body.

David wondered if Agent Cameron would have a 'show me yours and I'll show you mine' mentality. They might have come all this way for nothing.

"Doctor Kurov?" David lowered himself into a leather chair and placed the brown paper bag on the table. The chair hugged him, almost caressed him—budget well spent. What they lacked in security, they made up for in furniture. With how Operation Mindwarp turned out, Genesis might have been better off investing in furniture too.

Blake plopped down and instantly played finger drums. "We have everything you need up here," Blake pointed at his head. "You understand we can't take classified intel out of the building."

"I presume General Korhonen briefed us on everything you already know." Jia leaned back in her chair and rocked spastically back and forth like she'd downed a pot of coffee. "In layman's terms, Prometheus hates AI and wants it gone. They've never committed a criminal act in pursuit of that end, at least on the record. Never came up on our watchlist. You can imagine how many small pockets of groups like this exist that have a similar theme. From what we can tell of its founding members, they're a collection of technologists, ethicists, and former AI developers. I.E. they're well funded. None of the members have a criminal record." There was a long pause before Jia said, "Specifically, they are concerned about the creation of autonomous, super-intelligent AI systems."

"Any link to Bloomington University?" David said.

"At least two of their members completed research at Bloomington. Don't get excited though, because based on the people who regularly access Prometheus computer networks, they have about fifty-nine members. Of those we can identify, there are as many links to Berkeley and UCLA as there are to Bloomington, and they all have engineering departments. We can't search them all. And we have no concrete leads that any of them might be the target. The number of companies involved in AI research is massive. AIDA would have been our first choice, given their ties to the US military. You know what happened there."

Blake and David gave each other a disheartened glance.

"And you don't think we're just early?" Blake said. "And the bomb isn't there yet?"

Agent Cameron released the file in his hand to scratch his short, curly hair. "We have local PD in their jurisdictions looking at last known addresses. Everyone we've interviewed seemed horrified and confused by the idea of being involved in terrorism. Everyone is singing, but nobody knows the right song."

"The only suspect we have is Doctor Kurov. We need her to talk," Jia said.

"We've moved Doctor Kurov to an interview room." Agent Cameron checked his watch. "You'll have about twenty minutes with her before we have to prepare her for transport. We can meet back here when you're done. Of course, we'll be listening in on the other end."

"Alright, let's jet."

David and Blake followed the agents down a flight of stairs to an interview room, where they watched Doctor Kurov from the other side of a one-way viewing mirror. She sat on a hard plastic chair, her hands shackled to the table. A few dark bruises had popped up on the side of her face like someone had hit her with a flat object—they really didn't care to hide what they're doing at this point. Her chin rested on her chest as if she was sleeping.

"Find out anything new?" David asked, the bag in his hand crinkling as he pulled out the beer and chicken salad.

"I don't think you have time for lunch," Agent Cameron said.

"She does."

***

The moment he opened the door, the cold in Doctor Kurov's eyes melted.

"Beer and chicken salad?" She sounded amused and disbelieving. "You came all the way here to bring me that, Dreamcatcher?"

David sat and placed the beer and salad in front of her. "I asked if you wanted anything. Only polite of me to get it for you."

She studied him for a moment before cracking open the lid. The fork came up like a weapon in her hand. "They let you arm me?"

"I've been extensively trained in fork-to-hand combat."

Doctor Kurov launched into the salad. Her face nearly pressed into the food as she shoved it down her throat like she hadn't been fed in days. Maybe she hadn't. "I didn't like how our last talk ended. You apologized for lying to me. Why did you?"

"Lie or apologize?" she asked with a mouth full of food, not the slightest concern for how she looked with food falling out of her mouth.

"Lie," he said.

"Time."

"You were buying time? So I wouldn't search through the rest of your dreams?" Had they missed something after all? Blake didn't think so. "Or so you could move the bomb into place?"

She twisted the cap off the beer and chugged down half of it before she paused. A good amount had spilled out of her mouth and dripped down her shirt. She didn't reply until she finished her meal and tapped the end of the bottle for every drop. "What happened to the man that raped your sister?"

David froze. They both knew agents were listening on the other side of the window.

"Lena, I need us to focus on the bomb before it's too late."

"We are. What did you do to the person who raped your sister? He killed her, right? The guy that raped her? Might as well have wrapped that cord around her neck and pulled. Do you dream about it? She'd be alive if it wasn't for him."

"If our parents were different. If I paid more attention…" David gave himself a long blink to clear his thoughts. "A lot of things that day could have gone differently."

"Did you want to kill him?" she asked.

Keep it professional. This conversation is being recorded by the FBI.

"David? Did you want to kill him?"

A knock came from the door, and David reached for the knob like a lifeline. He pulled only enough to reveal Jia on the other side mouthing the words "*Need help?*" Did he need help? If he nodded and Jia came in, their conversation would become formal and Doctor Kurov would freeze back up. Not accepting Jia's help would force him to keep the conversation going, hoping to take it somewhere useful. *Doctor Kurov better not be stalling for time.* The clock in the room read ten thirty-six, and they expected the DHS at ten forty-five.

David shook his head and closed the door.

With his eyes still on the door, David said, "I wanted to kill him, sure. I was sixteen years old. Too young to know what was really happening."

"You tried, didn't you? You went to him intending to kill him. Something stopped you. What was it?" Her chains rattled as she shimmied her chair toward him.

A lump formed in David's throat he needed to squash. "He beat me half to death. The guy was twenty and much larger and stronger than I was. A few weeks in the hospital killed my taste for revenge. I couldn't attend her funeral. My mother recorded it for me, and both my parents stood beside me as I watched the video. My dad made sure I knew how he felt about missing my only sister's funeral just to take a beating."

David turned, took two steps toward her, and kneeled. "It's what you're trying to do. Revenge for the family that needlessly died that day. You blame yourself. Because you programmed the AI that led to their death. That's why you're letting these people beat you. You're not fighting to stay strong to ensure the bomb goes off. It's your penance. You think you deserve this."

The glare from the light shined on her face, highlighting several bruises and a few partially healed cuts. She paled and breathed faster. Her breath smelled like beer. David craved one.

"Do you want to be the person someone else is going to kill for?" David pressed, his voice intensifying. "Someone's mother, daughter, sister, best friend? Is that how you want to be remembered? Because they're going to put your face all over the news. The Prometheus Guild won't even be a footnote." The FBI certainly would have made that exact threat to her during a session of good cop, but they hadn't built a relationship with her. It hadn't been personal when they said it. David hoped it was enough.

She stiffened. "You'd let them blame me? I'm not doing this alone."

"It's not up to me. By all records, I'm not even here. I know you're hurting. What happened was terrible and they should be held accountable. The technology might not be ready. Someone can investigate what happened. People don't have to die."

"They knew the technology wasn't ready. The bastards went ahead with its implementation, anyway. They knew, David. And they covered it up. Do you know what the news printed? A gas explosion. They didn't even have gas pipes in their fucking home. Do you know what the reporters said when I confronted them about that? They said their focus right now is on the victims and the community's recovery."

Her lips moved like she was going to say more, when the door burst open and a broad-shouldered female and thin man, both wearing dark suits, entered the room. "Time's up," the woman said, her voice deep and hostile, confident in a way he'd only ever heard from Blake. She brushed past David and gripped Doctor Kurov's hands so hard she cried out.

"She was going to say something," David said.

The women released the chains and shoved Doctor Kurov into the other man's arms, then stepped up to David. She was half a foot taller and wider. "Didn't she already tell you where the bomb is?"

David opened his mouth to protest, then closed it. This woman wasn't being paid to listen. It's not how she operated. *Another hammer. This one, too, looks like a sledge.*

"Tell me," David shouted after Doctor Kurov as they dragged her out of the room. He thought he saw tears running down her cheeks, but they pulled her out of sight.

"I told you. The last time I said goodbye," she said as her voice faded down the hallway.

David marched to Agent Cameron and grabbed him by the scruff of his shirt and shoved him against the wall. "You couldn't buy me a few more minutes? She was going to tell me. I know it."

"Captain, it's been a tough couple of days for all of us. Now, you're going to release me and we're going to walk out of here peacefully, or you're going to spend a day in lockup."

Blake touched David's shoulder. "Not his fault."

"He could have stopped it," David said, turning his head to look at Blake. "You would have knocked him out already."

Blake grinned. "And I would have spent the day in lockup. Not your style."

David eased his grip on Agent Cameron. Jia stepped between them as if Agent Cameron needed a shield.

"Time to go. It's over," she said, her words infused with both empathy and resolve.

"She was going to tell me," David whispered twice more, not quite believing the DHS would strong-arm him at a moment like that.

"Or she's sending you on another useless chase to buy time for Prometheus." Jia guided David out of the interview room and to the boardroom. Blake and Agent Cameron followed behind. None said a word to each other.

The chair didn't seem as comfortable as it had thirty minutes ago. David couldn't stop thinking about what Doctor Kurov might have said if the DHS hadn't stepped in. *She was going to tell me.* He'd never know if he would have learned the truth and found the bomb. Maybe she'd tell the DHS after all, and they'd find it. Credit didn't matter to him, he just wanted people safe.

"She said she already told you where the bomb was." Blake interrupted his thoughts.

"Is she referring to AIDA?" Jia asked.

David shrugged. "She must be. It's the only location she gave me." He couldn't think of any other location she'd hinted at. He'd done a lot of the talking, hoping opening up to her would create a bond between them.

A knock at the boardroom door drew all their attention. Another agent stepped in and dropped a pair of glasses on the table. David froze. "What are those for?" The glasses looked like a replica of the 3D glasses he'd seen in the trash in Kurov's office. The same ones in her dream on the desk.

"Thank you, Geoff," Agent Cameron said to the agent that had dropped them off. He picked up the glasses and put them on as he glanced out the window.

Blake frowned at David. "What, the eclipse glasses?"

Chapter 13

David reached for the eclipse glasses when Agent Cameron offered them. All their eyes had fallen on him.

"Are you okay, Cap?"

"David?" Blake said.

I know where the bomb is. Part of him wanted to tell the agents sitting a few feet away. Why not hand off the responsibility? *Because they won't believe me. They're tired of me guessing.* Although he was almost certain he knew where the bomb was, he'd been this certain before and was wrong. Twice. "If we're done here?" David said. "Master Chief, let's jet. It's a long way home. When is the eclipse again?"

Blake eyed him for a moment, then stood.

"In a couple of hours," Agent Cameron said. "Half the office will be watching. Are you sure everything is okay, Captain?"

David felt sweat dripping down his arms. "Yeah, sorry. Just realizing I've neglected my family. They're off this week on holidays. I should be with them." Helen had said she was going to take the boys somewhere special to watch the eclipse, that one of the universities had a kids' event planned.

Jia followed them out of the building. David sensed Blake ready to burst at the seams, but he kept his mouth shut until they reached the car. As they drove out of the compound, Blake asked, "What is it?"

"The last words Doctor Kurov said to me at Genesis was 'Keep your head up, because for a moment as brief as a heartbeat, the world will change.' I'd thought she was offering self-help advice. I think she might have given me the time the bomb goes off." David gripped the wheel as he sped down the road. He checked his watch. "Do you have your phone with you?"

Blake pulled out his phone and waved it like a flag of surrender.

"Search up Bloomington University and the eclipse."

"The eclipse? You think—"

"Just do it." He pulled out his own phone and called Helen. "Shit. She's not answering." He handed Blake his phone and said, "Text her and ask her where she's watching the eclipse from." *She wouldn't go to Bloomington. She wouldn't.*

Blake sent the text, then went to work, tapping away with his phone. It took everything for David not to stop the car and run the search himself. They might not have time. If David was right, Prometheus would have the bomb in place, right in time for the eclipse. The bomb wasn't targeting a building or a lab. It was targeting an event.

"Fuck, why didn't you say something to the FBI?" Blake said.

"What? What did you find?"

"An article from the university about the eclipse. The president of the university marked the eclipse as a celebration of technological advancement. Listen to this quote from the university's paper: 'Just as an eclipse represents a rare and awe-inspiring alignment in nature, we view this breakthrough in AI as a pivotal moment in the alignment of technology and human capability.' Wouldn't someone at the FBI have caught that? Jesus."

"The university is the target. Where are they gathering for the eclipse?"

David could barely stand waiting for Blake to read through the details. He tapped his phone to bring up the lock screen, praying to see a text from Helen. Nothing. He couldn't slow the car. Every second counted.

"They have a large amphitheater that holds a few thousand people. And I bet there's a stage where the university president is giving a speech," Blake said. "A place the FBI never would have thought to check."

Blake dropped his hand into his lap. "You want to call the FBI?"

"Not yet. I don't even know if they'll listen. We've burned those bridges. And I don't have any proof. Just a really strong feeling." David glanced at Blake, and they both smirked.

Blake shook his head, but there was a hint of respect in his smile. "You figured it out. And you didn't have to hurt her to do it. It was the right call to put you in charge." He opened the glove box and pulled out a Sig Sauer M18. He dropped the magazine, scanned it, and popped it back in. David knew it would have seventeen rounds—he checked it regularly. "Do you have another one of these hidden in the car?" Blake asked.

"Just the one."

"Mind if I hold on to it?" Blake's eyes practically sparkled with anticipation.

Blake hadn't been out of Delta Force that long, and not only did he have superior weapon skills to David's, he wasn't afraid to use those skills. Hesitation would be dangerous and David's instinct was to talk them down, show empathy.

They pulled onto the Bloomington University campus. Security blocked the road, waving people into a parking structure not dissimilar from the three-story parking garage at Genesis. For a moment, David thought maybe the FBI had figured out the bomb was there, but then he saw crowds of people down the street, lined up beside a building. Blake directed David to park down the road, six blocks away from campus. With his phone, Blake scrolled through the map, deciding on the best approach angle to the stage. He'd had plenty of time to study the map while David drove. Since Blake had led assault teams in combat, David agreed with all his suggestions, as they all made sense.

"Keep in mind that no battle plan survives contact with the enemy," Blake said after they completed their plan and shoved David's gun into the back of his pants, using his shirt to cover it. "As things go wrong, stay close and follow my commands, okay?"

"As things go wrong?" David frowned. "We're just getting eyes backstage, confirming the bomb, and calling Agent Cameron, right?"

Blake smiled. "Right. And when that simple plan goes to shit, stay close and follow my commands."

"Copy," David said with a passive shrug. Let the hammer think about the nails.

David had expected to catch a lot of glances from university students curious what two old men were doing walking down the road toward the amphitheater, wearing casual clothes and not the suits professors and staff members wore. Yet as they passed hoards of young people, eyes glazed over them with as much care as an iceberg for a sinking ship. "What's the going age here?" David said.

"These days? All ages."

"I guess we can't rely on Prometheus standing out in the crowd," David said, tugging his shirt away from his sweaty chest. He already had a shaded patch on it.

When they rounded the building where the crowd had been, a large sign noted the eclipse gathering with a date and time, special guests, a firework's show, and a band. "That's why it's jammed," David said. "They're doing it all." He glanced at his cell. Still nothing from Helen.

He called her again, got her answering machine, and left a message for her to call him back right away.

"Prometheus won't stand out here." Blake marched past the stage to the back of the amphitheater where several large trucks were parked in two lines. Drivers stood all around—at least David assumed they were all truck drivers because of their enormous bellies and the constant flashing of their phones, presumably checking the time. They'd want to know how long they'd been there and how much longer before they were off the clock. Drivers didn't get paid by the hour. They were paid by the load. This delay would turn disgruntled quickly.

One driver saw Blake and gave a chin nod to a man standing beside him. All eyes in the driveway drifted to Blake and David, as if they'd been waiting for someone in charge.

"Unloading?" Blake smiled, stepped up to the driver as if he was in charge, and shook his hand enthusiastically. "Anyone unload yet?"

The driver leaned back and raised his chin, acting superior to Blake. If Blake noticed, he pretended he hadn't.

"The last truck unloaded about thirty minutes ago. Ain't seen no one from the university to direct this mess since then. Can't drive down the damn street with all these people here."

"Thirty minutes? Is the last truck to unload still here?" Blake asked.

The driver pointed at a small five-ton truck, out of place given the larger semis backed up on the road. The five-ton had no driver inside. David walked over and peeked in the back. The box was open and empty.

"Can you move this along? I'm hungry. Haven't eaten in hours," the driver said, getting many nods of approval from the other drivers, as if they were all starved.

"I'm on it," Blake said, patting the driver on the shoulder. "We'll get you out of here in no time. I'm going to go inside and check on the driver."

An open door led to an abandoned path beneath the stage. David expected to see campus security, given that the FBI had just searched one of their buildings for a bomb, but the entrance was a free-for-all. Blake walked ahead of David, nearly pressed against the wall, his pistol gripped tightly in his hand and waiting for a reason to squeeze the trigger.

David felt his phone vibrate in his pocket.

Hey babe, at Bloomington University. They have everything here! Face paint, cartoon tattoos. You okay?

"Oh no." His mouth dried and his hands shook. A sudden, overwhelming terror froze him. Blake turned, looking at his hand, then his eyes.

"What is it?"

David swallowed hard, unsure if he could force the words out. "Helen. She's here."

Blake took David by the shoulders. "Take a couple of breaths. Let's get focused on disarming this thing so nobody gets hurt, okay? You need tunnel vision."

David couldn't even comprehend Blake's words, never mind follow the commands. He texted back: *Get out of here. Now.*

Blake shook David, more aggressively this time. "Come on."

"I can't just not think about it," David snapped at Blake. "I'm not like you." He re-checked his phone several times, trying to refresh as if it would force her to answer faster.

"Stay here if you need to. I'm going to confirm the bomb."

David grimaced. He couldn't let Blake go in alone.

A large double-door was propped open at the mid-point of the stage. Blake poked his head around the corner, signalled two fingers, and pointed inside. *Two targets.* He turned the corner with his pistol raised and stepped out of David's visual. David paused, waited. He didn't have a gun of his own, so he wouldn't be helpful.

"Down on the ground," Blake said, barely loud enough for David to hear. "Don't. It's not worth dying for."

They definitely believe it's worth dying for. David risked a glance and saw two men lying facedown. He creeped inside and saw the security guard that probably belonged on duty at the entrance. The guard didn't move, and there was a small pool of blood next to his head.

"FBI?" David whispered.

Blake shook his head. "Call them. But we can't wait for them to get here. We need to get eyes on the bomb. If they know we know, they might set it off early and kill as many people as they can."

David heard the crowd outside in the field and knew Blake was right. They had to secure the bomb and pray it wasn't on a remote detonator.

"Find something to tie these two. I'm moving ahead," Blake said, immediately stepping further into the dark recesses of the stage.

David whispered to Blake. "Where? Where am I going to find rope?"

Blake had already turned the next corner.

Other than a few stacks of chairs and a dozen sets of empty lockers, there was nothing in the room. Not a single strand of rope and definitely no convenient packages of zip ties. David had just started to punch 9-1-1 into his phone since he didn't have the FBI number when one man on the floor got to his knees, as if sensing David was out of his element and didn't have a gun. The other man raised his head and smiled, realizing the same thing.

"Shut it down," David snapped, his tone brooking no argument. The threat of force could be as powerful as the use of force.

Both men thought about it, then gave each other a smile and stood simultaneously. One was much shorter than the other. Both had muscle comparative to swimming noodles, but that didn't make them less dangerous.

"Get down on the ground," David hissed. No longer on the hunt for rope, he was now on the hunt for something to defend himself with. He'd done some hand-to-hand combat during basic training, but he was no fighter. His weapon search was as successful as his binding search. He nearly called out for Blake on instinct, holding back as the words almost escaped his lips. *Damnit, Blake. No shitty battle plan execution survives contact with the enemy.* "I won't tell you again," David said. He'd lost any control he might have had. They both stalked toward him, their faces filled with rage. He also noticed their hands made no movement for a device in their pocket, which meant these two were mere goons. *Someone else has the detonator...if there is one.*

The shorter man froze. "I'm going to stop the other guy. You take care of this one."

The taller of the two men nodded and smiled as he cracked his knuckles and dug his feet into the dirt like a bull about to charge. *He is a bull about to charge.* The man ran at David with giant hands outstretched like a wrestler aiming to grab hold and throw him into the nearest set of lockers. The noise wouldn't be enough to cause someone outside to get help. *Nobody is going to hear me get my brains bashed in.* With a three-foot gap separating David from his attacker, he took two quick steps forward. Then, David dropped and kicked out the man's legs. The man's momentum carried forward, his legs no longer beneath him, and he dropped like a baseball player sliding into home base.

When the man got to his knees, David seized his shoulders and drove his head into the nearest locker with a resonating boom. Three more slams and David let him drop, confident he wouldn't rise again.

A gunshot cracked around the corner. David sprinted in the direction Blake had disappeared, heart pounding with each step. The shorter man lay motionless on the floor. No visible blood yet—either it hadn't pooled or the sandy floor had drunk it in. Twelve paces away, Blake had his arm locked around a third man's throat while the man thrashed against his grip.

"Status?" Blake's forearms bulged with effort as the man's struggles weakened. Then his eyes rolled back in his head and he slumped to the ground.

"I couldn't find any fucking rope," David yelled.

"These guys look familiar?"

"The one there," David pointed at Blake's feet, "was in her dream, welcoming her to Prometheus. Don't recognize the other two."

"And that crate?"

David eyed a crate pressed against the wall, its height reaching his waist. All sides looked tightly sealed. "This must be it."

"Did you call the FBI?" Blake asked.

David checked his phone. A message from Helen read *leaving.* "What do we do? Get as far away from here as we can?"

"Should we get an evacuation going?" Blake asked.

"If someone is watching and can detonate remotely, they'll do it when they see people leaving."

Blake nodded as he raised his phone to his ear. "Agent Cameron. Tell him we secured the bomb and need a team here to disarm it. Bloomington University Amphitheater."

Chapter 14

David sat at on a gurney, pressing a pack of ice to his head while a paramedic hovered nearby. Flashing emergency lights made his head hurt, and he closed his eyes to the light show the FBI had created on campus. Hundreds of students hovered nearby, oblivious to the fact that if the bomb had gone off, they could all be dead. The FBI may have created what they thought was a safe barrier, but it was possible a large piece of concrete could fly across campus and hit them. Dozens of phones pointed in their direction, getting good footage of the commotion. The Prometheus Guild would get a lot of attention, even if the FBI disarmed the bomb. *It hadn't been for nothing, Doctor Kurov.*

"Good work, Cap," Jia said, a lightness in her voice he hadn't heard before.

"Thanks. Still don't have them all in custody."

"Count it as a win. Finding the others falls on us now. Bomb squad's finished their work—they're moving it out. Because of you both, thousands get to live. Just want you to know that when Agent Cameron comes down on you for going in on your own." She patted David on the shoulder. "He's pissed about that."

David laughed and looked at Blake. "I was assigned a hammer for a reason."

Her nose scrunched up, but she chuckled and walked away.

"Agent?" David asked before she could get too far. "What's going to happen to Doctor Kurov?"

Jia sighed, her smile fading. "DHS will make sure she's prosecuted. Doubtful she'll get the death penalty, though there's a good chance she'll get life in prison."

"Even though she's the reason we disarmed the bomb?" David asked.

"I'm not a lawyer, but her cryptic cooperation isn't going to save her. If Genesis hadn't been involved and you hadn't deciphered her message, a lot of people would be dead."

David gave a curt nod. His family had been there. If not for this assignment, he might have been in the audience with them. The biggest success of his career and it felt hollow. David would be in prison too, if Marcus hadn't beaten him half to death when he tried to get revenge for his sister. Even after the beating, while laying in the hospital bed, David thought about finding a gun and shooting the bastard. It took so long to recover he'd lost the will to fight and Marcus skipped town. Somewhere deep inside, David still wanted revenge for his sister. It would be so easy to look up Marcus and ruin his life the way he ruined David's family. *So why did I choose differently? What makes Doctor Kurov different from me?*

"You good, David?" Blake sat next to him. "Long face for a guy that successfully completed his first mission as a lead and saved a few thousand lives. Thousands of families won't be mourning tonight. Many won't even know any different."

Lead. He hadn't done a lot of leading. Blake and Isaac knew their jobs. A day ago, the FBI wanted to crucify him. And mission success? That depended on how General Korhonen measured it.

David couldn't get Doctor Kurov out of his mind. He should have helped her. He kept silent, unable or unwilling to talk about it because Blake wouldn't understand. Blake was built different. He was a hammer.

***

David shook Esmeralda Rodriguez's hand. "It's nice to meet you." He sat on a velvet chair opposite her and set the file he'd brought with him on the coffee table, beyond her grasp.

"Call me Esme," she smiled. Her thick lips and boisterous brown hair suited her job as a Los Angeles Times reporter. She'd agreed to meet with him at the Palm & Vine, a luxury hotel on the outskirts of LA, suited to corporate getaways orchestrated by businesses like Ashley Madison. If Helen checked his credit card, she'd be furious, had he not already told her his plans.

"Esme," David said. "I appreciate you taking the time."

"Very clandestine, coming to a place like this." She scanned the room, as if hoping she might spot someone important she could use to put together a scandal. Why not make her trip even more worthwhile? Normally, people like her weren't welcome inside the hotel unless invited. "Your email alluded to a conspiracy? I usually ignore emails like yours, except it came from a DOD domain."

David knew it was the only way to get her attention. He also knew his email might have been flagged on the way over. But so far, none of his superiors at Genesis had asked about it. They'd be too late now. "Your guarantee?" he asked.

She giggled, covering her mouth like a high-schooler. Some people might have found her character charming, even alluring. David found her irritating.

Esme crossed her heart. "I swear if the information you have in that file is a proper conspiracy, it will be on the news tonight."

He slid the file over, ready to say goodbye to his career with the DOD. "And the credit for the story?"

Her eyes narrowed. "That, I don't understand. You want me to name the whistleblower…" She swiped the screen on her phone. "…Doctor Lena Kurov?"

"When you read the full story, you'll understand."

Esma took the folder. "Not a big talker, huh? Check the news at six if this is as hot as you make it sound." She stood, wiped the back of her skirt several times, and walked out the door.

David sipped his cold beer. He finally deserved one. The news had run a story about the incident at Bloomington, calling it a technical malfunction in the wiring that started a fire and required evacuation. No mention of the bomb. Tonight, though, they'd know the truth about Prometheus and Autonix: the guild had built a bomb using an AI intelligence designed to detect threat levels in a civilian population. Had the decibel level gotten much higher—the band coming on stage or another hundred people gathered—the AI would have detonated the bomb to end the terrorist threat.

The military wasn't ready for autonomous AI. Thanks to Doctor Kurov, the world would know it.

David thought about Doctor Kurov waiting in some DHS cell, enduring more interrogation while the story was being buried. He couldn't save her from prison, but he could make sure her truth wasn't lost beneath classified stamps and bureaucratic silence. Maybe this was how you really broke cycles of violence—not with more revenge, but by dragging dark things into the light.

"Would you like another beer, sir?" the waitress asked him.

"I'd love one."

Author Note

What started as a short story grew into one of my favorite novellas. I loved diving into David's character, uncovering his family dynamics, and exploring how his background made him uniquely suited to the project.

The idea for this story came to me while brainstorming at my desk. I wondered: what if we could solve crimes before they happened—while they were still being planned? If we could enter the dreams of terrorists, could we effectively stop their future plots? And what would the government do with such a tool?

While I didn't fully dive into all the implications of these questions, it was thrilling to explore them at a high level.

Acknowledgements

Many incredible people helped make this novella possible.

To Ayden Rails, my developmental and copy editor: Your insights and feedback continually elevate my stories. This book is what it is today because of your expertise and dedication.

To my alpha and beta readers—Ione Jayawardena, Ludmilla Dubuisson, and Nikki Kennedy: Your thoughtful feedback and encouragement make every book stronger. I'm deeply grateful for your guidance and support.

Finally, to my Kickstarter backers: Your belief in *The Genesis Project* made this novella a reality. Your support means more to me than words can express.

Book Review

If you enjoyed this book, please consider leaving a book review. It means the world to Mark and helps other people find his books. As an indie author, it's essential to getting noticed online. Without a massive marketing budget, an indie author's next best resource is reviews.

Thank you so much.

What's Next?

Want to experience the haunting mission that shaped Corporal Anthony Hodge? Witness how a routine sniper operation becomes a devastating moral crucible when a young soldier must decide between duty and conscience.
[FREE Download]

***

Step into a mission where following orders and saving innocent lives collide. Join Echo team as Captain James Burmann makes a fateful decision that will haunt his unit.
[FREE Download]

About the Author

Mark PJ Nadon writes pulse-pounding thrillers that dive into the darker corners of the human experience, where ordinary people are tested by extraordinary circumstances. Drawing from his service in the Canadian Reserves, he crafts stories that blend intense action with psychological depth, taking readers from apocalyptic wastelands to dystopian futures, and even into vivid fantasy realms. His work reflects a powerful belief: while darkness shapes us, it doesn't have to define us. While not writing, Mark lives in Ottawa with his son Matthew and K9 Rocket, runs a fitness company and embraces adventure through rock climbing.